I0450834

KRAKEN ME

APART

Mainely Monsters #1

Alex Silver

CONTENTS

Synopsis

When I threw a ring into the ocean, I was only humoring my best buddy's weird superstitions. But now it turns out that one of the monsters he wanted to protect me from thinks we're mates. Being accidentally married to a kraken is one thing, but the more I get to know Kirby, the less I can resist his strange charms—or his tentacles.

CHAPTER 1

Wherein Tristan makes an offering to the sea

S alt spray wets the rocks as I step outside my spacious two-bedroom home and onto the pebble-strewn stretch of desolate beachfront that's all mine as of today. It's surreal standing on my own little patch of shoreline and looking out into the choppy bay full of jagged rocks cupped between two crags.

Pine trees along the ridge obscure the view of my nearest neighbors. I can almost imagine I'm the only person for miles out here. It's peaceful, the roar of the surf and the occasional calls of sea birds the only noises, a beautiful music all their own.

Another sound thrums along, harmonizing with the current. It reminds me of the haunting whale song from the PBS documentaries I watch sometimes when I can't get to sleep on my nights off. Working overnights screws with my sleep schedule something awful. I must be overtired if I really think a whale is singing to me. If there are any whales out beyond the arms of the bay, I can't differentiate their splashing from the choppy waves.

It's gorgeous out here as sunset kisses the surf, setting the ocean awash in warm colors. The cliffs cupping the cove make it less than ideal for swimming. My realtor warned me the undertow here is nothing to mess around with. The local rumor-mill calls this Devil's Cove and everyone knows my new home's previous owner, Craig Delmare, drowned here. And the swirling superstitions about his house are the only reason I could afford such prime coastal real estate.

Hoyt, my best friend, insists that my nearest neighbors are now sirens and sea serpents. But I'm pretty sure Craig drowned without any mythical intervention. I stand there, enthralled by the slowly sinking sun, until I hear a car approaching. That has to be my best friend, coming to celebrate.

I'm not normally one to be bothered by solitude, but I'm glad when I see Hoyt's headlights rounding the bend in the road and approaching my driveway. Hoyt parks behind my car and steps out with a huge grin on his face. He holds up a gift bag from the nice little import wine shop on Main Street. It still blows my mind that I could afford this place. Right on the water and minutes from the touristy resort town where I work at the local hospital.

"Congrats, Mr. Homeowner." Hoyt pokes my ribs and thrusts the bag into my hands. I grin back at him and open my gift, eager as a kid at Christmas.

"Thanks, I still can't believe it. This place is amazing!" I pull out a bottle of my favorite cheap sparkling wine and an expensive jar of caviar I've joked about trying someday. I glance into my buddy's grinning face. "Seriously?"

"Hey, we always said we'd try that crap when we make it big. And buddy, have you ever arrived!" Hoyt arches a brow and sweeps a hand toward my new digs. And yeah, I can't argue with that. Success feels good.

"Cheers, share this with me?" I offer, not ready to be alone out here after dark.

"Obviously. Bet it tastes like those slimy tentacles you're into. Can't wait to see you get your first taste," Hoyt teases.

"Hey!" I flush, but he's not wrong. That is a definite part of the appeal. Hoyt knows enough about my alien fantasies that it's pointless to deny how often

I've contemplated what it would be like to have a tentacle actually fucking my throat. Doesn't mean I want to share that experience with Hoyt. "Now I don't want to try it with you." I pout at him, arms crossed over my chest.

"Sure you do. You want to lap up all that slimy sea goodness. I'm not sure how we're supposed to eat it though, like, do we put it on a cracker?" Hoyt mimes shoveling the cured fish eggs onto a cracker. He's so bouncy, dark curls flopping into his bright blue eyes as he talks, and I can't even pretend to be upset with his entirely true teasing.

"Clearly, this calls for the good silver." I put my presents back in the bag so I'll have a free hand. We both turn toward my house. Pride swells in my chest like a party balloon as we approach my first proper home.

"Oh yeah, clearly. If only you had any." Hoyt rolls his eyes at me, knowing that I don't own good silver, or any silver at all.

"Hey! Who says I didn't get some? Bet it would keep your ex away if I had real silver. You know, hipster Cory? With the protein power balls and the furry face and the silver allergy?"

"Oh, Cory," Hoyt says his ex's name wistfully. He gives me his most enigmatic smile, the mischievous one that all but screams he knows something I don't. Instead of shaking his head at my ignorance and spilling some heretofore unknown secret, he winks lasciviously at me. "Wildly codependent, but he certainly had some tasty balls. Silver wouldn't have kept him away; he was terrible about his allergies. That boy had the scariest reaction to peanuts and I can't tell you how many times I had to throw out peanut-butter-flavored snacks he brought over with him."

"I remember, you called me panicking to talk you through how to give him his EpiPen."

"Yep. Scary shit. Don't worry though, Cory hasn't come sniffing around in ages." Hoyt still looks unduly amused as we talk about his ex.

"Yeah, but for a while there, I thought the breakup would never stick. How many times did you have to remind him you weren't dating anymore?" I ask.

"Only twice. So less than your record with that closeted hockey jock in our first year at UMaine. Remember him?"

"In my defense, his hockey chirps served him well in bed. The dirty talk was on point until I realized he really had a complex about being gay." I sigh.

The guy really dug into my humiliation kink in bed, too bad he was a total ass to me out of bed too. Never got the memo that just because I loved being called a filthy slut while he fucked me didn't mean I wanted to be treated like a dirty secret. We saw each other off and on for several months before I got totally fed up with being his emotional punching bag to work through his self-hatred. Hoyt was there for me through the entire torrid affair, reminding me I should hold out for kinky, hot sex *and* respect from the guy I was banging.

Hoyt hums a few bars of "Toxic" at me. I roll my eyes. Rehashing our lackluster love lives is familiar territory, but I am looking forward to celebrating our bright futures tonight, so I change the subject.

"Come on, we can find something to pair this with inside. My realtor sent over a charcuterie plate and one of those fruit bouquets to celebrate; you might as well help me eat that too." I sling an arm around Hoyt's shoulders to guide him into my house. He veers toward the beach with a strange look on his face. I know he's going to spout more of his superstitions at me before he even opens his mouth.

"Sure, but first I want to show you something. There's no sense in taking any chances. If you really have sirens in the bay, you'll want to give them an offering."

"Really?" I arch a brow at him, not sure whether to be exasperated at his insistence or touched by his genuine concern.

Hoyt has always been into cryptids. Ever since we got bullied for reading one too many Bigfoot stories at school. Well, that and my general weirdness. In response, I did my best to mask my autism. Then I went into a field that lets me explore a special interest without having to deal with the public and their judgments most of the time. Hoyt doubled down on the gossip about his weirdness, starting a lucrative local tour business that takes people out searching for monsters of myth and legend.

"You never know, there's still so much we haven't explored in the depths of the ocean," Hoyt points out. And he's not wrong. I just don't believe that magical singing merfolk are among the wonders waiting to be discovered.

"What if I want a sea monster lover to explore my depths?" I tease him.

"I know you do. Remember who bought your first tentacle dildo when you were too chicken to do it? Humor me anyway?" The pleading in his voice sways me more than anything. He pouts like he's only playing, but his bright eyes pinch with genuine concern for me that warms my heart, even if he is being ridiculous with his strange beliefs. "I mean, if they're a mere local legend, no harm, no foul. But if there's even a slight chance of them singing you out of your bed and onto their dinner menu..."

I hesitate with another denial on the tip of my tongue. Then again, if it would put his mind at ease, where's the harm?

"I want you to be safe, Tris. Please?" Damn, he bats his concerned eyes at me and I relent.

I sigh. "Fine, make your offering, I guess."

Hoyt pulls a small satin pouch out of his pocket, grabs my hand, and dumps a gaudy silver ring onto my palm. He curls my fingers around the smooth metal that's warm with his body heat. "It doesn't work that way. *You* live here, so it has to be from you."

"Fine." I huff out an impatient breath, but restrain myself from rolling my eyes at him. The sooner I get this over with, the sooner we can celebrate. And if I appease Hoyt's weirdness, I might convince my jumpy subconscious there's nothing ominous lurking under the waves. "What do I do?"

"Well, there are a few protective rites that I found. But this one is supposed to be the strongest. You just have to pledge yourself to the sea. If you're already symbolically one with the tides, they can't lure you away to join them."

I give him a skeptical glance, but Hoyt seems entirely serious. I sigh, resigned to doing whatever he asks next. "Ugh, fine! I'll do it if it will get you off my back with this siren nonsense."

"Perfect! Here." Hoyt proffers his Leatherman and I glower at him.

"What do I need that for, Hoyt?"

"You have to offer your blood for a true binding. The call of the sea within you blending with the sea without, obviously. Come to the water."

I follow him reluctantly. Something about the crash of the waves sounds too much like the strange whale song I heard before he arrived. There's nothing watching us; it defies reason to think there is. But it can't hurt to take every precaution. Hoyt doesn't stop until we are standing in the surf. My shoes are going to be ruined.

Before I can protest, Hoyt takes my hand and pricks the tip of my finger with his knife. At least he didn't slash open my palm like we're in some cheesy as fuck horror movie.

"Ow!" I try to yank away from him. Hoyt holds tight, smearing the drop of blood that wells up from the pinprick wound onto the tarnished silver of the ring before he releases his iron grip on my hand. I scowl when he lets me suck the stinging injury into my mouth. The coppery tang of blood turns my stomach, but it soothes the sting. "Anything else?"

"Yep, hold still. Good thing you need a trim anyway." Hoyt snips a lock of my sandy brown hair from behind my ear where it will be less noticeable at least. He knots it through the ring before pressing it back into my hand. "Now cup it in your hand, blow on it, and repeat after me: blood of my blood, breath of my breath, protect me from a watery death."

I raise an eyebrow at him. "Really?"

"Just say it," Hoyt prompts, gesturing for me to get on with it. "Then give it to the waves."

So I repeat his ridiculous mantra and when he gestures like he's throwing a frisbee, I skip the bloody ring into the waves. It's probably my imagination that I see something gliding up from the depths to catch it. Pure fantasy that I hear several echoing splashes all out of proportion with the plunk of the trinket sinking beneath the waves.

There wasn't nearly enough blood to produce the reddish purple swirl of something that could be a jewel-toned human-sized tail cutting right below the surface. Or is it a sea snake as thick around as my waist? That's far too fantastical to be real. I blink away the image. I must be seeing things, reading into the last fading glow of sunset. There is nothing lurking beneath the ocean's surface when I look back.

The last sliver of sun sinks below the horizon. Darkness blankets the waves, turning the ocean into a churning abyss that swallows the light of the twinkling stars. I shudder and shake off the strange sense of gazing into a void that could swallow me whole without even noticing. I have to be imagining the eerie certainty that the void is watching me back.

Still, there is something haunting about the evening birdsong over the crash of waves. I can't shake the idea there's something gazing at me from the ocean's depths. Hoyt's been getting into my head with his superstitious nonsense. He will never let it go if I admit to nerves about the cove though, so I pointedly turn my back on the dark water.

"There, now you'll be safe." Hoyt slaps my back, like we accomplished some important task. I glance at him, and when I glance back over my shoulder at the water, there's nothing there. My pulse settles into a slower tempo. Nothing out there can hurt me in my cozy little house. Hoyt is putting ridiculous notions in my head with his tall tales. "Let's toast to your happy future here."

"I'm good with that." I nod.

Hoyt slings an arm around my shoulders and we pick our way back up the rocky beach and inside to celebrate. The wine is sweet, and the caviar smells like the sea, and tastes of sharp, clean brine. It pops when I bite down, the savory iodine flavor of the ocean filling my senses in a surprisingly pleasant gush. It sort of reminds me of going down on a sexy guy. There's something sensual about rolling the little balls around in my mouth. It grows on me more with every spoonful.

Hoyt grimaces and spits his mouthful into the trash.

"More for me," I joke.

"You're welcome to it. I can think of better things to put in my mouth." He makes a face and pours himself another glass of sparkling wine. He reaches for a pineapple from the fruit arrangement with a leer.

We finish the bottle of wine and both end up falling asleep on my couch. It's a good way to christen my new home, filling it with laughter and companionship. And if I'm a little lonely thinking about spending future nights alone in the big echoing house, surrounded by the sounds of the sea? Well, I'll just have to make a habit of entertaining my friends. I have plenty of space for it now.

CHAPTER 2

Don't krill my vibe

The new house is starting to seem like home after a few weeks. I've finally got a night off to stay in and relax with no need to unpack and organize. Working the night shift means not being awake or available when most of the world is around for socializing. That's something I consider a perk of the job. I've always been a bit of a homebody and small talk is awkward. I have a few people, like Hoyt and my sister Caroline, who I am close to, and that's enough for me.

My most recent ex got so frustrated with me over date nights. I've always preferred dinner and a movie on the couch over going to a club or bar, or even eating at a restaurant. That was the last straw on his long list of reasons I was too weird to love. I would far rather be comfortable in my own space than deal with the bright lights and noise of most public venues.

Hoyt insists that I date the wrong people. It's gotten to the point I've contemplated giving up on romance, except I crave companionship. Most of the time, I'm content with inviting over friends like Hoyt. But some days it would be really nice if I had a boyfriend to snuggle next to on the couch, and maybe have it lead to more.

Sometimes, all alone in my bed, I miss being wrapped up in a lover's embrace with a powerful yearning. I was unprepared for how much more intense that drive has gotten since I moved here. I always pictured myself putting down roots with a man I love by my side.

Someday I'll find a lover who can look past my hang-ups about everything. Like the way the lightbulbs flicker at the grocery store that's closer to home, so I have to shop at the one on the other side of town to avoid a meltdown. And how it's not worth it to go out when I know the loud noises and crowds at most date-night venues make my skin itch with the need to hide in a dark room for hours afterward. The way I fidget out my nerves. Or how picky I am with my food. And how I can talk for hours about my favorite alien romances, but lack patience for a five-minute conversation about the weather.

But while I'm waiting for my prince charming to stop dicking around and dick me down, I have a selection of dildos and porn to get me by.

Tonight, after taking advantage of my time off by sleeping in for a few hours, I'm still cozy in my bed with nowhere to be. I roll over to pull out a selection of my favorite toys from my nightstand drawer. Lube, a cock ring, and my two favorite tentacle toys all go on top of the nightstand within easy reach. I linger over the tidy coils of rope. I'm too horny and impatient to fuss with bondage that will inevitably leave me wishing for a lover to tie me up for real.

The fundamental problem with restraining myself versus playing with a partner is that I always know I have full control over releasing myself. It mutes the sense of helplessness I long for. The padded cuffs have the same issue, though they're quicker and more convenient than the ropes. I ignore both options and make sure the lube is in easy reach, then cue up my new favorite monster fucker scene on my audiobook app.

Sometimes I watch porn, but most of the sexy grunting and groaning is comically overdone, even in my favorite bondage videos, and it's hard to find good tentacle porn. So I usually rely on finding hot monster scenes from my audiobooks to help me go to town with my giant fake monster cocks.

The newest hit from Anita T. Enticle—subtle, she is not—features an alien covered in an improbable number of tentacles. I have been thoroughly enjoying listening to him boning his way across the galaxy. It's written in first person, so it's really easy to let the words wash over me and pretend I'm really being held firm in some massive monster's thrall. Forced to take his cock like a good little slut.

Perks of not having any nearby neighbors, I can stream the scene to the bluetooth speaker on my dresser. Gone are my days of worrying about dislodging an earbud at an inopportune moment. The sexy rumble of the narrator's bass is so much clearer this way as the alien describes his bound and naked lover fingering himself. Mm. I get comfortable, stretching out on top of my blankets.

My smutty book almost drowns out the sounds of the local seabirds and the waves lapping at the shore outside. Actually, that's louder than usual today. Did I accidentally leave my window open?

I glance over to check. Yep, the blackout curtain is shoved back enough to reveal a narrow strip of the gauzy valence beneath. Both curtains move in a stray breeze. I consider getting up to close it, but it's still warm enough not to bother when I am horny as fuck and have more pressing matters on my mind.

I shove down my pants to rub my stiff cock, turned on at the idea of someone wanting to linger outside and listen to me getting off. In the abstract, it's hot to think about it. The locals avoided this strip of beach even before my home's previous owner walked into the ocean, never to be seen again. And it's not like the sirens Hoyt keeps teasing me about are real. So having a secret voyeur watching through the window will remain a sexy fantasy instead of a terrifying reality.

I want this to last, so I ease my cock and balls through a stretchy silicone ring, settling the attached vibrator just behind my sac for later. I roll a condom over the flexible length of shimmery purple silicon for easier cleanup. Then I slick it with lube. In preparation for taking the toy, I finger myself open.

"You're going to take every inch of me like the needy little slut you are," Throgdar, the sexy alien, growls over the speakers.

I push the tip of the toy against my rim, mimicking the way the narrator describes the alien opening up his human lover. My breathing hitches and I could swear I sense eyes on my exposed skin. But there is no one around for miles, unless shrieking gulls count.

"No! It's too much, I can't!" Eric, the other protagonist, protests.

I don't think I'd say no to the sexy muscle-bound alien pinning me in place with his tentacles and penetrating my hole so thoroughly I saw stars. But getting called a slut just does it for me.

"Fuck, hold still." Throgdar slaps Eric's ass.

Ngh, I bite my lip, relishing the sting of pain and vaguely wishing I had someone to swat my ass until it's suffused in that warm glow of pleasure-pain. Eric is one lucky bastard. It's not the same when I try to smack myself. I can't ever seem to get the right angle.

In lieu of a spanking, I fuck the first few inches of my toy into my ass more forcefully. It's narrower at the tip, quickly flaring out to roughly the girth of a soda can. The molded suckers scrape deliciously over my rim, and I moan as I press it deeper.

"Stars, you're begging for it, aren't you, slut?" Throgdar's deep voice demands, and I pretend he's talking to me, a shiver going down my spine at how intense the big alien is.

"Mhm," I moan, writhing on my bed until the springs creak as I open myself up more.

I can almost imagine I hear the crunch of gravel from outside. As if my imagined watcher is really standing there, appreciating the view, his feet shifting as he palms his stiff dick. Too excited at the sight of me splayed open before him to wait a second longer.

The bed creaks under me as I spread my legs wider—likely the actual cause of the indistinct sounds. I want to give my pretend voyeur a good view. Fuck, his imaginary eyes burn against my tender hole. I plant my feet on the mattress and thrust the toy in more forcefully, not sure whether the voice on the audio track or my imaginary guest has me hotter. It doesn't matter. The need to be stretched and experience the heat of being filled to my limits consumes me, leaving me burning with lust.

"I need to feel you! Yes, give it to me harder," Eric cries.

"I am going to stuff this needy hole until it's ready to burst," Throgdar growls over the speaker. I tune out Eric's response.

"Ungh." Yeah, that's exactly what I want; some big beefcake pounding into me and leaving my hole gaping when he's done with me.

I might have no one to fuck me at the moment, but what I've got to work with is a truly epic silicon tentacle dick. I work it deeper, fucking myself mercilessly. The porn alien narrates all the inventive ways he's going to dominate and debase his human lover.

I'm getting close, so I turn on the vibrating cock ring and press it against my taint. The way it squeezes me is a tiny glimpse of how the alien's tentacles wrap around Eric. They have barbs that latch onto his flesh and leave him covered in what amounts to dozens of tiny love bites. The narrator talks about lines of welts marring Eric's skin. I bite my lip, wondering what the tender little souvenirs would feel like.

Fuck, that's good. Distantly, I hear the squelching of the lube in my ass echoed outside. My voyeur jerking himself off to the sight of me stuffed full of tentacle dick. Fuck. I want to watch him paint the siding in his release from spying on me as I come my brains out.

I want to be filled even more. It's not enough to forget that I'm the one doing this to myself. I fumble next to me for the other dildo I set aside earlier so I can shove it past my lips. I suck on it, imagining Throgdar's thick appendages impaling me and holding me in place. He wouldn't let me move as he sucks his marks into my skin, spilling his alien seed inside of me, choking me on his tentacles and fucking me on his cock.

Over the speakers, Throgdar comes inside his human and there is a brief pause between chapters. In that lull, I could swear I really hear rustling outside my window. It must be the curtain swaying in the breeze, or an issue with the recording I never noticed before.

My breathing grows ragged from the effort of fucking myself from both ends. I glance at the window. I can see outside through the sheer valance when the darker curtain billows inward. A vague outline of someone staring inside startles me. The curve of a head peers at me, two luminous eyes fastened on the toy tentacle I have shoved up my ass.

I jerk upright, spearing myself more firmly and gagging as I inhale sharply around the cock in my mouth. The sensation of choking and having the toy rammed against my prostate, even as the vibrator sends electric tingles through my balls, is too much to take any longer.

I have to be hallucinating those strange eyes meeting mine through the window. Not enough oxygen as I gag on the silicon cock shoved down my throat or something. It's got to be my overactive imagination spinning a shadow of the shrubbery into something as alien as Throgdar watching me.

The low hum of the ocean's ambient sound seems to crescendo into a roar of white noise. Not my name. Not a command to come, whispered in a voice that sounds like the sea. My vision narrows as my orgasm crashes over me.

Oh fuck, my balls draw up and I shoot convulsively over my lower belly. The tentacle toy is rammed so deep it feels like it might merge with my body. As if it might take on a life of its own and wreck me the way I long to be used.

My dick spurts again as I frantically jerk myself through the orgasm, one last valiant little dribble of cum oozing down my shaft and over my fingers. When my breathing evens out and my heart stops racing, I realize I probably need to make sure no one was actually creeping around outside my house.

With a disgruntled little groan, I turn off the vibrations before oversensitivity strikes. I ease the tentacle free of my hole, strip off the condom, and plunk it onto the side table. I drop the cock I had in my mouth next to it to wash both toys later. Mess dealt with for now, I pad my way to the window, just to be sure I'm not really dealing with some sort of sexual predator.

I give myself the space of two deep breaths to prepare for whatever is out there. I sweep the curtains aside, throw open the pane, and lean out, hoping to startle any intruder into fleeing. The shrubs sway in a gentle breeze.

No one is out there. Not in the bushes, not on the expanse of dry autumn grass that sweeps down to the rocky beach. Certainly not standing on the gravel pathway that leads from my patio to the sea. Not a soul in sight. My racing pulse eases back out of the stratosphere.

"Is someone there?" I call into the still evening air. My voice doesn't even shake. I sound like a badass. Or like I just came my brain out to monster fucker porn. Hopefully, I didn't give my voyeur any weird ideas.

I shiver at the thought of some unseen person slipping into my room and playing out my wildest imaginings with me. I'm pretty sure the half-chub I'm sporting from the thought of it would shrink into my body if it actually happened. Fantasies are wild like that.

I shake my head at myself. There isn't anyone watching me. And no one wants to bend me over, pin me down, and fuck me seven ways from Sunday.

The sun is barely a sliver on the horizon and the beach before me is desolate and bare. The only sign of life is a gull that squawks in my general direction. It takes a shit, as if to say fuck off, before winging up to the cliffs where a whole flock of the creatures has taken up residence. If not for the noise and the epic amounts of poop they leave streaking the cliffs, they'd be the perfect neighbors. Well, that and making off with some food I left unattended the other night when I had the bright idea of grilling on the beach. If I'm honest, attended food isn't much safer from their predations.

I shouldn't be disappointed that no one violated my privacy. I just... was certain I sensed another presence while I was getting off. Must have been my vivid imagination playing tricks again.

I've been feeling eyes on me anytime I go outside ever since I moved in. So maybe Hoyt is playing some sort of long con on me. That would make sense in his ongoing campaign to get me to believe his nonsense theories about sea creatures coming for me in the night. Or I'm letting my imagination run wild. It's only been a few weeks. I'm still getting used to the solitude out here.

I latch the window lock again, and draw the blackout curtains to block all traces of anything that might inspire another flight of fancy. Then I turn away from it to clean my toys. If I'm only getting that one tentacle, I might as well make the most of it.

I ignore the hairs prickling at the back of my neck as I turn away. Even with the window firmly latched, I catch a few notes of the eerie whale song that always seems to drift up from the bay in the evening. It's nothing. Nothing but actual whales.

CHAPTER 3

Don't cause a comm-ocean

"Hey, you're into weird science, right?" Brad asks during a lull between new med orders from the emergency room. Usually the ER dictates how busy we are overnight since most of the other docs get their orders in and get out of here during the day shift.

Brad is the only technician working with me tonight. Which is usually fine for a Wednesday. The pimple-faced college kid has been working the overnight shift with me since he started at the local private college a month ago.

He has far too much energy for someone burning the candle at both ends. I'm not sure how he manages our hours and his course load, but it's none of my business as long as he does his job. Normally, I'm perfectly happy for work to be quiet. Which means that Brad's talkative personality tries my patience.

I don't glance up from the medication orders I'm verifying. He's supposed to be drawing up single-dose syringes of oral Tylenol since the third floor is running low, but the kid needs constant reminding to stay on task.

"That order isn't going to fill itself." I nod toward his work.

Brad hurriedly gets back to the monotonous task, but that doesn't stop his mouth from running. "Well? Is it true that you go out into the woods hunting Bigfoot in your spare time?"

"No." I clench my jaw and pull up the next patient chart. That's a rumor from my misspent youth that has more to do with being so close with Hoyt.

I don't have the patience for chitchat or correcting the record. As much as being lumped in with conspiracy theorists bothers me, I'm more upset when people are mocking or dismissive toward my friend and his weird superstitions.

Luckily—for me, not the patient—the ER just called down that they admitted a middle-aged local guy to intensive care. He'll be getting an ICU bed to recover in once he comes out of emergency surgery for an animal bite and he needs IV vancomycin. Hospital protocol means that I'm in charge of calculating the dosing for the antibiotic. So that's going to keep me too busy for chitchat with Brad.

"Sorry, I can't talk right now. Grab the vanco dosing folder for me?" I point at the big orange binder where we keep all the paperwork for the medication protocol. I print out the calculation sheet and set to work inputting the new patient's lab values. Brad unobtrusively sets the binder on my desk and returns to his work. The kid can at least read a room sometimes.

I could do the familiar math in my sleep, but not paying attention is how errors get through to patients. Brad's incessant chatter can't distract me. I triple-check the dose calculation based on our patient's reduced creatinine clearance and put through the order. Since Brad isn't trained on making IVs yet, I'll have to actually draw it up too.

I sigh as I push back from my workstation to handle the urgent order. It would be nice if we had full ER coverage, but I'm slightly spoiled from working in the city during my training. Out in the wilds of rural Maine, we make do. Even in the nicer coastal towns, where the tourists bring an influx of cash each summer.

"Where are you going?" Brad asks.

"I've got a stat order for vancomycin." I gesture with the label as I pick it up off the printer.

"Oh, another one?" Brad grimaces. "How many weird animal attacks does that make this month? Lucky the tourists haven't caught wind, huh?"

I scowl at him. "You make it sound like there's a wild animal rampaging through town."

Brad shrugs laconically. "All I'm saying is, if I *did* go out hunting monsters for fun, I'd be extra careful lately. I've been hearing shit, man. And it's the full moon, so I'd be careful around anyone coming in with bite marks this time of month, you know?"

He mimes howling at the moon, then shudders dramatically. "Better safe than furry."

"Sure." I roll my eyes at him. Because, of course, the kid buys into all the ridiculous lore Hoyt is obsessed with. As if werewolves are a common occurrence, wandering around Bellweather, biting unsuspecting tourists.

"Just saying." Brad turns back to his work. He hums along to the music playing through the single earbud I let him wear to balance my sanity with being able to get the kid's attention.

"Sure. I'm going to go make that IV for Mr. Allen. Have a batch of those ready to take up to the third floor when I'm done, got it?" I level the kid with a no-nonsense look and he gives me an infuriatingly cheeky salute.

"Sure thing, doc." Brad pops his second earbud in as I leave. It's not worth reminding him we agreed to keeping one ear open or that the title is unnecessary.

When I glance over at him as I'm scrubbing up to make the IV, he's jamming out to his music. I shake my head ruefully. At least he's doing the task I gave him; I'll pick my battles. And I might linger a little more meticulously than usual as I work under the sterile hood to make the medication. Not enough to delay our patient getting his first dose, just enough to be thorough—and milk out the time I can avoid my chatty co-worker.

When I'm done, I tap Brad's shoulder. He startles, yanking the bud out of one ear and flailing his arms to keep his balance when his chair tips back onto all four legs.

"Can you take this up to the ICU?" I hold out the palm-sized bag of clear liquid. It's so tiny for something so potentially life-saving.

"Yeah, sure thing, wolfman needs his antibiotics." Brad winks at me as he takes the IV bag. "Oh, hey! Don't some things we carry contain silver? Is that on the drop-down menu for allergies you showed me when I'm doing med rec?"

I pinch the bridge of my nose and breathe through my irritation with the kid's antics. "You won't be doing any medication reconciliation with Mr. Allen. He's still under anesthesia at the moment." I don't dignify his wild guesses about silver allergies with a reply. I answer the underlying question since at least he's showing some initiative, and unlike werewolves, metal allergies are real. "And you're right. We stock some silver-containing wound care products since it has antimicrobial properties. So if a patient reports a metal allergy, you can and should flag it in their profile."

"Cool. Be right back, boss." He winks at me as he grabs the IV bag. "Those are ready for you to check." He points at the full bin of single-dose oral syringes, whistling to himself as he strolls out of the pharmacy. I sigh as I sit down to verify his work. It's going to be a long night.

CHAPTER 4

Marri(n)ed at first sight/acci-tenticly mated

Whirp I leave the pharmacy, dawn is barely cracking the horizon. The full moon set ages ago. As overnight staff, I have a reserved spot close to the hospital's emergency department entrance. It's not quite as nice as the priority spots in the well-lit parking garage where I used to work, but it's a small town.

Brad's shift ended before mine, so he's long gone as I turn the engine over, shivering in the late autumn chill off the ocean.

It seems extra cold tonight. Which reminds me of Hoyt. He had a private cryptid hunt last night, if I recall correctly. I sit in the driver's seat, waiting for my car to warm up. My car's bluetooth connects to my phone and on an impulse, I give Hoyt a call.

The phone rings for long enough that I start to worry that I'm waking him up. And then longer still. It rings until I'm worried about finding my best friend next to Mr. Allen in the trauma ward. Both of them recovering from a mauling by monsters I don't truly believe exist.

My patient's chart lists a canine attack as his chief complaint. He got seriously wounded. Bitten badly enough to require emergency surgery. It's an unfortunate accident, but nothing more sinister than that. Judging from how long he was in the OR, I'm guessing whatever dog bit him had a set of jaws. But at worst, it might have been a pack of coyotes. Nothing paranormal or that I need to worry about.

Right before Hoyt's voicemail would pick up, he answers. His gravelly tenor rumbles through my car speakers and sends a surge of relief through my body. He's perfectly fine.

"Yeah?" Hoyt grunts.

"Hey, Hoyt."

There's a long beat of silence. "Who's dying?"

"No one."

There's another beat of silence.

"Did you finally get dicked down by an absolutely hung alien lover sometime last night?"

"Um, no."

"Uh huh. So why are you calling me at the butt crack of dawn when you know I had a job last night?"

"Um..."

"Did you forget most folks are still in bed when you crawl out of your work dungeon again?" There's a hint of humor under his exasperation. So I probably didn't actually wake the man up.

"No." Maybe a little. But I also know he wasn't in bed. If he was on a hunt last night, he's got to be just wrapping up work too. "How was the monster hunting?"

"Oh, I see what this is. Shucks, Tris." Hoyt guffaws, the sound echoing and crackling in my speakers. "Are you calling because you were worried about little ol' me?"

"No! Of course not. I know you can take care of yourself." He's the scrappiest fighter I've ever met, and that was before his brief stint in the military. If anyone can take care of himself, it's Hoyt.

"Damn right." Hoyt snorts. "Anyway, the hunt was a bust. Usually is when I've got a clumsy greenhorn tagging along, stepping on every twig and sending every rock clattering."

"Was the client upset?"

Hoyt chuckles. "Come on, Tristan. I know my business better than that by now. We saw what he paid to see, and he left satisfied."

"You paid an actor to leave some footprints or something?"

I can practically hear his unconcerned shrug. "It's not a con if I've actually seen prints in the area. I have a casting of the genuine article."

"Sure you do." I roll my eyes. The work makes him happy, and it's not my business what gullible tourists with more money than sense waste their cash on. Hoyt sells an experience and our lawyer buddy Galen assures us that, legally speaking, his business is entirely above-board. People pay for what Hoyt delivers, real or not.

"Someday you'll see what's right in front of you, Tris."

"Right now, all I see is the hospital parking lot. Not a monster in sight."

"Uh huh. Whatever you say. So, did you really call to make sure I got home alright?"

"We had another animal attack come in."

"Ah. So you really were worried? I'm flattered."

"Knock it off. The victim is in the ICU this time. Brad is convinced it was werewolves. He's started wearing this gaudy silver charm bracelet with enough religious charms on it to be the setup for a bad joke."

Hoyt chuckles again. "I'd like to see that."

"No, you wouldn't. This kid would drive you bonkers."

Hoyt snorts. "He certainly gets under your skin. So, why did you call me, then?"

"To tell you to be safe out there."

"Sure. You too, man. I'm home, unwinding before bed. Where are you?"

"I'm leaving work."

"Well, drive carefully and text me when you get home. Watch out for that turn near Devil's Cove."

I roll my eyes and put my car in gear now that it's toasty warm inside.

"I'll go slow, but it's not like it's quite cold enough for ice yet."

"It's not the ice I'm worried about, Tris."

I roll my eyes. "Even if there *were* hypothetically real sirens in the bay, you realize that I'm not even a little bisexual, right?"

"Is there even such a thing as a little bi? Either you like multiple genders or you don't. Regardless, where do you think baby sirens come from? Just because people didn't discuss the males doesn't mean they don't exist."

"I don't know. I don't normally speculate on mythical monster reproduction."

"Oh, sure. Unless it involves tentacles."

"Hey!"

"You know it's true. Anyway, tentacles or not, I suppose a lack of daddy sirens could be why they lure their human victims to themselves. But even if they have human fathers, surely all the baby sirens aren't girls."

"Or—and I'm still not saying I believe any of this nonsense—but if they're all women like the stories imply, there's always parthenogenesis?" I suggest distractedly. I let go of the amorphous anxiety that made me call Hoyt and relax into enjoying the familiar banter with my friend.

As I pull out of the hospital lot and drive along the eerily empty predawn streets, I spot a pair of joggers in neon lycra. I lift my hand in a wave as I pass, recognizing one of them as a nurse from work. I'm tempted to warn them about whatever has been stalking the woods, but that would be paranoid. Cathy knows about the weird surge in animal bite admissions we've had lately, she'll be fine.

"Hm, I suppose." Hoyt pops the top on a can of soda and sighs as he settles into his easy chair. I can picture him getting comfortable. "So, you think they're part reptile?"

"Could be? That makes as much sense as fish people. Although they've documented parthenogenesis in several fish species as well. Are you going to stay on the line with me until I get home?" I ask, warmed by his concern for me.

"Uh huh, how else am I going to hear a siren's song without risking my life?" Hoyt teases before taking a noisy slurp of his soda.

"Ah, I see. You're totally using me and not making sure I get home safe at all, right?"

"Exactly. Did I tell you about the contract I got to search for a very particular mothman specimen?"

"Nope."

"They were interested in sightings of Rosy Maple mothmen. I explained we are technically within the actual insect's range, but Luna moths are more commonly found in the area and equally impressive. But apparently only a neon pink mothman will do. He simply had to check them off his bucket list."

I snort. "Cryptid gotta catch 'em all?"

"Something like that. Yeah. It was a little weird. I can't guarantee a find like that, but it's a mothman, they can go where they want..." Hoyt says. He keeps talking about his difficult client. I let his venting wash over me. I don't believe there are any mothmen flying through the predawn skies, but he does, so I listen and ask questions to keep him talking. He eventually steers the conversation into teasing me about my tentacle obsession.

Bantering with Hoyt keeps me occupied as I get to the final sharp turn to my home. It leads right up to the bridge over the inlet to Devil's Cove. Just like always, there's not a single sign of sirens. No irresistible music, no ethereal beauties lounging on the sharp rocks. Nothing.

I pull into my driveway and hang up on Hoyt. He plays up being disappointed about the lack of monster sightings on my commute. He wishes me a good night. I get out of the car and freeze in my tracks at the glimpse of motion near the shore. My heart leaps into my throat as the movement resolves into a gull.

I laugh off my nerves. It was only a sea bird taking flight. It calls to its flock as it wings up to where they roost on the cliffs around the bay. I try to convince myself the sense of eyes on me is nothing. The low rush of sound that evokes heavy breathing behind me is the ocean. Nothing more sinister than that.

Except the ocean can't explain why my back door is ajar, banging against the jamb in a stiff breeze. Fear curdles in my stomach, but I dismiss it. I probably just forgot to latch it properly on my way to work last night.

No big deal. It makes sense, since I was juggling my work badge, keys, and travel mug when I left. I let myself inside and hang my keys on their hook before turning and slipping on something viscous.

I land hard on my ass in a puddle of sticky-slick goo. It smells briny, like the ocean, and a glistening trail of it leads from my mudroom and into my house. When I try to get up, I slip and slide until I have to plant my hands in the goo to push up to my feet. It feels like the slime my eight-year-old nephew, Lyle, is obsessed with. The thick mucus coats my floor and pants, and drips from my hands.

I wipe the disgusting snot-like strands of sticky mess off onto my soaked pants. At the back of my mind I can't help wondering if Hoyt's sirens really are real. What else but their doomed singing could possess me to do anything other than getting back in my car and heading in the opposite direction of whatever left that slime trail?

Except I don't really believe this can be anything other than a prank. What could possibly leave a human-sized slime trail through my house? Nothing. There is absolutely no rational explanation for it.

So Hoyt must be playing tricks on me. I pull my phone out of my soggy pocket, dry it as best I can on my shirt and text him to say I'm safe inside. I half expect him to call, crowing that he got me good with the slime. After a brief pause, Hoyt sends a thumbs up. Okay then. He's playing it coy; I can do the same. No need to reveal that his little prank still has my heart racing.

Keeping my shoes on to protect my feet from the goo, I shuffle-skate my way along the trail. It leads through my kitchen where I wrap my phone in a dishcloth to let it dry and keep it out of the mess. I glide further down the hall to my bedroom.

At first, my eyes skate past what I see there waiting for me. There's a hunched figure standing over my bed. No, not standing. There aren't any legs and whatever that thing is, it isn't human.

My brain can't comprehend the shape in front of me, looming in a dripping puddle of the same thick goo I'm covered in from my fall. I stand in the doorway staring as the thing turns toward me, goat-like eyes fix on my face. A strange bird-like beak clacks as the creature chitters loudly. Then it charges me in a tangle of undulating limbs. It looks like nothing so much as those videos of octopodes swimming along the ocean floor, tentacles writhing over each other in a hypnotic tangle.

A scream catches in my throat as a mass of snakelike appendages propels the creature toward me. I'm frozen in fear. Which is just as well, considering the slick puddle I'm standing in means that I'd only fall on my ass again if I fled in terror like any reasonable person should. Before I can so much as open my mouth to let out my shriek of terror, something whips out and grabs my ankles, coiling around me and toppling me over. I flinch, closing my eyes and bracing for an impact with the ground that never comes.

More thick coils wrap around me, not letting me move as they hold me aloft. My arms are pinned to my body, all of me wrapped up tight. How many appendages does this thing have? And oh my gosh, am I having some sort of lucid dream? This is the start of countless fantasy scenarios, and even though I'm terrified, I'm also uncomfortably turned on by the crushing grip around my torso.

I don't really want to see death coming for me, so I hang there at the monster's mercy, awaiting my grisly fate. Eyes shut tight against the horror holding me captive. My heart is racing, my belly still caught in a giddy swoop somewhere between terror and delight. It's like the plunge at the start of a roller coaster, except I'm not entirely sure the car isn't about to launch me right off the tracks, figuratively speaking. And fuck me if that edge of danger and uncertainty doesn't add to the appeal of being wrapped in tentacles.

The creature holds me there, and the reality of being bound in a tentacled embrace is even better than my fantasies. Nothing inanimate could squeeze with this perfect balance between immobilizing me without hurting me. The limbs holding me are slick with more of that slime, but they're also unmistakably alive, pulsing with heat and sinuous muscle. Ugh, I shouldn't be enjoying this, but there is something wonderful about getting to live out my lust-fueled daydreams. Too bad it might be the last thing I do. I'm still not sure whether the tentacles holding me captive in their alien embrace are about to feed me into a gaping, hungry maw.

Except instead of being devoured alive, I'm hyperaware of body-hot slime dripping onto me as the thing snuffles over my face. Something hard and smooth nudges against my nose and I crack open one eyelid, only to recoil at a goat-like eyeball the size of my fist inches from my own.

The creature squawks at me, nictitating membranes flickering over its strange, swirling pupil as it contracts. That eye is oddly compelling as I stare directly into it. Oh fuck, this is really happening and I might be about to die. Icy dread squeezes around my heart, as unyielding as the tentacles gripping me.

The creature lets out another unearthly wail and I finally find my voice enough to cry out, only for a sucker lined tentacle to slap over my mouth.

"Are you my mate?" The words sound strange and garbled coming from a beak. They don't make any sense.

I gape at him, shocked. There's no way this tentacled intruder is my mate. It can't be anything except a figment of my imagination—albeit one that has somehow tapped into my deepest fantasies.

"Mmph." I mumble into the tentacle covering my mouth. When I part my lips, the tip of it dips inside, probing my gums and cheek. It presses too firmly for me to even consider biting down. As if I have enough of a death wish to piss off whatever this thing is.

More of the same briny slime from the entryway oozes into my mouth. I gag at the strange viscosity coating my throat, but the flavor is weirdly nice. It has a clean ocean note, like the caviar Hoyt splurged on to celebrate my home purchase. The tickling sensation awakens some long quiescent instinct to suck on the intruding appendage.

"Pretty mate," the creature repeats, filling my mouth and caressing my cheeks.

I find myself suckling on the tip of the tentacle even as another of the ones wrapped around my torso explores my body. It starts to push at my slime-soaked pants, and part of me likes the idea of removing the uncomfortably damp fabric.

Except, the tip of the creature's tentacle is wriggling under my waistband and caressing my lower back and sending more dribbles of slime leaking along my crack. I get a mental image of that same appendage moving unerringly toward my pucker. Fucking me like no other and—no!

Nope, I'm not getting fresh with some sort of sea creature that hasn't so much as asked my name. A wild part of me that's bordering on hysterical connects that it is calling me its mate, so maybe it will respect my no? Fuck, I hope so. Fear and hope war inside me, waves of dread and desire mixing in a confusing cocktail.

"Nnnph!" I struggle, trying to spit out the thick length in my mouth and wriggling in its tight embrace.

The grip around my body loosens, and the tentacle withdraws from my mouth. It pulls away from my pants, the constriction around my torso loosening enough for me to gasp in a deep breath.

"I'm not your mate. What even are you? Let me go!" I sound almost as hysterical as I feel. None of this can be happening.

That big, strange eye swirls, and somehow, I think I might have hurt the creature's feelings. The world lurches as it spins me hastily upright. The creature steadies me on my feet before withdrawing all of its tentacles. It coils them under itself like some sort of horrific sea spider or a tangled ball of sea serpents. I shudder at the mental image. The creature squints enormous eyes at me.

"Mate?" it asks piteously. I take a better look, and okay, there is definitely nothing human about the creature in front of me. I am counting no less than eight tentacles, each of them thicker than my thighs where they merge into a central mass that seems to undulate with every nervous movement.

The monster's head is vaguely conical, with some sort of squishy crest that droops when it gives me a piteous look. Like it's begging. Absurd. Horrific sea monsters don't exist and they certainly don't beg like an overgrown puppy. They most definitely aren't somehow adorable.

"Um. I'm Tristan, but most of the guys who have tied me up and tried to get in my pants call me Tris. What's your name?" I don't expect an answer and I feel foolish for even talking to the thing. But at the least, it seems to know a handful of human words.

"Kirby."

I blink at Kirby. Kirby blinks at me.

"You're my mate. Krakens can tell these things. You left an offering."

"An offering?" I echo.

"Yes. A very fine mating gift." Kirby nods. One tentacle lifts from the balled up mass shifting nervously under the kraken and rises to show off a familiar, tarnished, gaudy as fuck thrift store ring. Kirby tentatively lifts one tentacle tip toward my hair, a match to the lock tied around the ring.

I blanch. Oh shit. I apparently made an unwitting proposal to a sea monster and it—he? If we're somehow mated, I hope the kraken is a he—said yes. Fuck my life. "No. I'm not your mate. Did you come from the ocean?"

"Yes. Where else would I live?" Kirby asks.

"I honestly have no idea."

I rub at my temples where a headache is brewing. Would Hoyt know what to do with a kraken? If he even believes me. No. I have to deal with Kirby, annul whatever mating he thinks I offered him, and move on with my life. I'll clear up the misunderstanding, send him back whence he came, and in the morning I can pretend this was a hallucination.

Maybe this all really is a contact high from the painkillers Brad spilled when he was drawing up more pre-filled oral syringes and forgot to cap a batch. Nevermind that the painkiller in question was only regular strength Tylenol. No, this is all too real.

"Tris?" I shiver at the way my name sounds, almost a breathy trilled song from that strange beak of his. And if I'm only hallucinating, is there really any harm in leaning into my mind's absurd conjurations? Why not feel one of those delicious tentacles pushing inside and....

Kirby's strange pupils get huge and his tentacles inch toward me. "You do wish to mate with me!"

"I, uh, what?" I try to will away my erection, because I shouldn't want to mate with this monster that broke into my house. Hell, Kirby shouldn't even exist.

"I can taste it. You wish to copulate." Kirby hunches a little closer, but he doesn't try to touch me again. And I can't truthfully deny that I am still turned on.

Well, fuck me sideways. And with Kirby, that's probably entirely possible in a literal sense, judging from the ease with which his muscular tentacles had me bound and gagged earlier. I shudder, and I want to tell myself it's revulsion at being violated, except apparently according to kraken society, I'm the one who came onto him?

I might break my brain if I try to think too deeply on that. If I'm honest with myself, I want him to wrap me in his inescapable strength again. I long to experience the powerlessness of being trapped without the terror of what he intends to do with me. It's hard to reconcile how turned on this entire encounter has me with the sheer strangeness of the night. It's surreal.

"I ..." I open and close my mouth, trying to find my words. "No. This is... I can't be your mate. I don't even know you. How are you even speaking?"

"I am an ancient creature of the deep; of course I can speak human tongues. You are fascinating creatures. How better to learn your ways than to watch humans through the ages? What else do you wish to know?"

"Everything? I don't even know your gender or your pronouns. Do krakens even have a gender?"

Kirby chortles, and his massive eyes crinkle in a semblance of human amusement. "I know of these human concepts. They do not concern me. We cannot spawn successfully together, so what difference does it make? You can use whatever pronouns for me will make you comfortable, my mate. He, based on your literary tastes."

"So, you're a dude kraken?" I swallow hard, mind flashing back to the unseen watcher when I was masturbating the other night. Was it him? Did he see how turned on I was over the idea of getting split open by an alien with similar anatomy to his?

"I am happy for you to view me that way, yes." Kirby's tentacles undulate around him and I stare at the hypnotic movements.

He's beautiful in a strangely compelling way, a ruddy dark purple. I'd never have believed I'd think that about a sea creature before standing here staring at him in my bedroom, dripping slime on my nice floors. But well, he's right. I *do* wonder what those strong tentacles can really do to me. Enough to let him show me.

"I can sense how much you wish to seal our mating," Kirby says, his tentacle tips twitching toward me before drawing back.

I can't deny the truth of his words. Despite his alien appearance, I want him. I have to be hallucinating if I think a horrifying sea creature from the deep is sexy, but fuck me if he isn't the sexiest person I've ever seen.

"So what if I do want that?" I ask, and it's so absurd, it's like I'm having an out-of-body experience, watching myself ask a literal kraken to fuck me. I lick more of his salty essence from my lips. He tastes good enough to lick directly from the source, and I'm obviously out of my head enough to want that.

"Then we can mate." Kirby moves several tentacles in something akin to a shrug. As if an interspecies mating is utterly mundane. I suppose it might be for sentient sea monsters. And with the embodiment of all my most vivid fantasies right there for the taking, I can't bring myself to care if it's taboo or wrong. Or if I'm actually concussed in a hospital bed and dreaming this entire encounter.

Kirby the kraken is offering me the dicking down of my dreams. Who am I to say no to a never in a lifetime offer like that?

I swallow hard and nod. Kirby puffs up his crest and considers me.

"Yes?"

"Yes." I nod again. "I want you to fuck me with your tentacles."

"Technically, these are my arms." Kirby waves them at me.

"Is sexy foreplay really the place for technicalities?" I cross my arms and pout at him.

"Excellent point, my mate. Allow me to ravage you with my tentacles to make it up to you?" He reaches toward me, and I reach back.

I'm ready to live my fantasy, if only for one day before I figure out what the hell kind of trouble Hoyt's little binding ritual got me into.

CHAPTER 5

Not a shellfish lover

My fingers tremble in anticipation of this first invited touch. Earlier, I was so startled by his presence in my room that I couldn't process what was going on, but now I'm hanging on his every move. Kirby twines the whip-thin tip of his tentacle around my wrist. I startle at the tickly sensations of his suckers latching softly to my skin. I squirm at how strange it is to have him pressed so close, almost like he's merging our flesh.

There's an incredible level of intimacy as he lifts the tentacle, drawing my arm above my head. And that's only the barest touch. I can't suppress a full body shudder at the mental image of all eight of his tentacle arms wrapped around my bare flesh in an embrace. It would feel like hundreds of little mouths, tenderly sucking on my skin.

Kirby notices my visceral response and pauses, leaving me caught in a delicious tension, with my arm stretched above me. "Are you well?"

He brings a thick tentacle up to coil against my forehead, as though he wants to check my temperature. How much human behavior has he observed over the years? Probably a lot, but his tenderness soothes away my uncertainties about this encounter. It makes him seem somehow less alien.

"I'm fine, just excited," I assure him, pushing his tentacle off my face with the hand he doesn't have pinned. Kirby absently loops another of his limbs around my wrist, drawing it up and out to stop me from interfering in his exploration of my face.

"Your skin is so warm," Kirby says.

His suckers cling so hard they pinch against my wrists. I whine low in my throat when another tentacle plunges into my pants. Oh fuck, I'm really getting fondled by a kraken. How is this my life right now? I'm so deeply into it I can't even bring myself to pretend otherwise.

"Your little tentacle is excited too," Kirby observes, wrapping around my dick in coils that have me gasping and panting his name. His touch is incredible.

"Kirby!"

I thrash in his hold, two more tentacles wind down my thighs toward my ankles, lifting me and holding me spread eagle before him. He collects the dripping precum from the tip of my cock with yet another tentacle and sucks the moisture into his mouth while I watch with parted lips.

"Mm, you taste like the sea." Kirby works my dick with an expertise I can hardly believe, exploring the tip with sensitive suckers like a dozen mouths sucking my length. I thrust helplessly into the relentless pleasure of his grip.

"Agh, please!" I'm not even sure what I'm pleading for. He's a feast for my senses and I want to savor every moment of this strange fever dream come to life.

"Hmm, you want a sample too?" Kirby asks, twining a tentacle along my jaw.

Before I can reply he pushes two thin tentacle tips past my lips. Kirby strokes all along the inside of my mouth before nuzzling his strange beak against my mouth. His tentacles cushion my tender lips against the strange hardness of his beak so that his tongue can tangle with mine in our version of a kiss. It's nothing like kissing another human, but his tongue does things to me. Things that send pleasure tingling through my balls. His salty sea tang is intoxicating as he explores every inch of my mouth, sharing our breath.

His strong tentacles hold me aloft, stripping off my pants and underwear, but not bothering with my shirt as they slip under the fabric. Kirby continues to pump my cock with a delicacy that belies his strength. If he's really a kraken, the terrifying stories of his kind imply that he could easily tear me apart. The powerful appendages that are currently pleasuring me to within an inch of my life could wreck me in terrible ways.

It's hard to believe this gentle giant would hurt a fly, but I'm acutely aware of the contained power underlying his tender caresses. The implacable strength when I writhe, trying to get enough friction to come. I'm hornier than I've ever been and desperate for release as Kirby's tentacles stroke over every bit of my exposed skin, milking my cock and massaging my arms and legs.

He wraps a coil around my chest too, more of his suckers finding and teasing my nipples. I lose track of time, kissing his beak as he withdraws one tentacle from my mouth to probe at my ass.

Kirby's tentacle pushes inside of me, thickening as he fucks me, unerringly finding the spot inside that sends lighting sparking along my cock. I moan into his mouth, but he swallows down my pleas with an unearthly humming song that vibrates through my entire body. Oh god, I'm going to come if he keeps that up.

A second tentacle probes my opening, pushing in alongside the first one. The two limbs work me in tandem, stretching me so wide I'm not sure I can take it. I definitely couldn't if not for his slime easing the way. Kirby's tentacles pulse in a delicious wave inside of me. He thickens the appendages as they pump deeper within my channel. His mouth on mine tastes of the clean brine of the ocean.

I'm getting more and more used to the smooth hardness of his beak on my lips, the firm musculature of his tongue tasting me. I struggle feebly in his grasp and Kirby moans another burst of whale song into my mouth that has me trembling with need. It's just as well that he's holding me up because I'm floating on the high of being entirely at my sea monster's mercy.

"Oh, fuck, please, I need to come so bad. Fuck me, Kirby. Mate. Fuck," I'm babbling and I know it, but I would say almost anything to keep experiencing the sheer bliss of this creature moving in and over my body. He ignites a lust so strong I've never experienced anything like it before.

This great terror of the deep is ancient and intelligent enough to communicate with another species. He can tear apart ships with his powerful limbs and all that intensity is focused on me. He's tearing me apart in the very best way and I'm going to burst if he keeps up the onslaught of pleasure.

I don't have words for what he is doing to me as yet another tentacle slithers over my tight balls. Kirby taps at the tender flesh where he's splitting me wide open, I can't take it. I buck and moan and empty my balls into the tight constriction of the tentacle that's still jerking me off.

"Come, Tristan. Give me your pleasure, my mate." Kirby purrs the words near my ear, and I am helpless to disobey.

I come like a fountain over his greedy coils. Kirby milks me dry. The thin tip of that third intrusive tentacle works my prostate from the inside even as he amps up the suction all along my shaft in pulsing pulls. His song vibrates deep in my bones as I come and come and come. My entire world reduces down to the kraken who is cracking my heart open in ways I never thought I'd get to experience. This is what it's like to be cherished by a lover who revels in bringing out my basest desires.

Kirby arranges me gently in my bed before hesitantly joining me, limbs curling around me until I'm cocooned in a protective ball of contented kraken. A combination of my long night, the intense orgasm, and his whale song purring lulls me to sleep, still wrapped in his tentacles.

CHAPTER 6

Safe(words) and sound(ing)

T he first thing I notice in the late afternoon sunlight streaming past the edge of my blackout curtains is that someone is holding me. Tight. Or perhaps more than one someone, because it seems like my entire torso is wrapped in bands of corded muscles.

"Ugh." My whole body feels leaden. It seems like a monumental effort to even reach for the alarm blaring on my bedside table.

My pre-dawn bedtime adventure comes back to me slowly as I realize I'm wrapped up in a sexy sea monster's tentacles. And he thinks I'm his mate. I try to rub at my temples, to dispel what has to be a lingering dream. Or hallucination. Is it possible there was a gas leak in the pharmacy last night? That might explain how exhausted I am.

But when I try to move, the delicate tip of one tentacle is coiled around my wrist, living proof that there really is a kraken in my bed. A living, breathing, tentacle covered lover. Holy shit. Somehow, the crushing pressure on my chest gets more intense and I can barely catch my breath.

There are actual tentacles immobilizing me even more thoroughly than in my wildest dreams. My real-life tentacled lover is clinging to me. As much as I'm unsure what I'm even doing and how I could have enjoyed getting fucked by someone so alien, I don't want to wake Kirby to have an existential crisis at him.

I work a hand loose to turn off the alarm so I can think this through. He squeezes me tighter, bringing my thoughts inexorably back to the sea creature in my bed. What have I done?

I mean, it's not like I went into the ocean and fucked some innocent, unwilling sea life. Kirby is clearly capable of making his own choices. And he didn't pressure me. Unless there's some sort of weird mating pheromone thing going on here? Because an amorphous sea blob that is ninety percent head and limbs isn't normally my preferred aesthetic in a partner.

Then again, it isn't *not* my preference either. It's only that I never imagined monsters or aliens or whatever he is could be real. But Kirby just...well, there's something about him.

Turns out a living embodiment of my most deeply seated fantasies has miraculously waltzed into my life. If that means looking past my accidental mate's strange appearance, at least it was fucking hot for him to hold me down and stuff me from both ends. All the while singing me the song of his people and milking my balls so dry that I don't know if I'll be able to come for a week. Unless it's from his tentacles invading my body again.

I groan, squirming at the ache from my hole. And Kirby's tentacles tighten around me. He makes another of those low, soothing whale sounds. The burst of exuberant song vibrates through my bones, echoey and haunting. It should jar me, but I take comfort in that low thrum of sound filling my chest.

"Morning, mate." His keratinous beak nuzzles into my neck. It feels like dozens of gentle hands are caressing me as he rubs his tentacles over my body. His suckers work over my skin in pulses of pressure. "Did you sleep well?"

"Uh, yeah, actually." I squirm at his ticklish touches.

"Good." Kirby circles the tip of one appendage over my half-hard dick, coaxing me to a full erection. "Do you wish to mate again?"

I swallow a denial; there's no point in playing coy. We've already established he can somehow taste my arousal and his touch is so good. I can't actually be his mate, but if I'm going to annul whatever this mating is anyway, I might as well enjoy the amazing sex while it lasts.

And maybe I should reconsider walking away from a lover who—oh! One of those slender tips is probing my tender hole, oozing his own natural slick. Kirby's movements fill my nose with the sharp tang of his clean, briny arousal scent. Vaguely, I wonder if his slime production is somehow sexual, since I didn't wake up in a puddle of kraken goo. That's a question for another time. I don't want to do anything to stop his tentacles from exploring my body again. One tentacle tip slips inside of me, leaving me whimpering and pushing back into him when he withdraws it. He's such a tease, and I love it.

"I didn't hear you, mate," Kirby taunts.

"Yes. Oh, fuck. Make me take all of you," I beg as he teases my cock and my hole in alternating touches.

Kirby makes an amused sound. The tentacle in my ass thickens and nudges against my prostate to send sparks of pleasure shooting through my balls as he undulates in just the right spot. "You think you can take all eight of my tentacles?"

He waves a thick coil in front of my face, filling me with a visceral thrill.

"No!" I shake my head. I absolutely cannot if they're all that thick. But fuck me if I don't want to try now.

"We will work up to it," Kirby suggests, several of his appendages stroking over every inch of my body. "I can make them miniscule until you are used to taking all of them at once."

He doesn't have to spell out that he can as easily make them very large and stretch me to my limits. That prospect has my dick aching with need and my hole clenching in anticipation of a thorough fucking.

His suckers pay particular attention to my most sensitive spots. It's like each of his eight limbs has a mind of its own, all of them hellbent on driving me wild with sensation. And actually, I recall something to that effect from my reading on real-life tentacle anatomy. If he's a close relation to octopi, anyway. Not that it matters when all eight of his limbs are working in tandem to edge me to within an inch of my life.

The tentacle wrapped around my cock squeezes, suckling all along my shaft in a rippling wave of suction, heat, and pressure. The one sealed over the tip of my cock coaxes me so close to the edge I'm afraid I might come before he gets a second tentacle inside of me.

That would be a crying shame. Good thing Kirby seems to read me like a neon glowing sign, because right before it all becomes too much, the sucker pops away from my tip. It tears away with a sting of pain that's the perfect amount to back me down from the edge of orgasm without doing any real damage.

I curl in on myself as much as Kirby's firm hold on my body allows and pant through the aching sting. Kirby adjusts his grip on me, freeing the thin tip of his tentacle to trace the faint red mark his sucker left on my cockhead. He thins his tentacle out, somehow going from a few inches around to no thicker than a pencil, and probes at my slit.

Lost in a haze of pleasure, I don't realize what he's about to do until a thick bead of his tentacle slime drips onto my cock. He nudges it into the tip of my dick.

"Is this okay?" Kirby asks, voice breathy.

He can't really mean... Oh fuck, he does. I've never done this before, but have I dreamed of it? Not with a cold, clinical rod, but a living, writhing invasion like he seems to want? Mm. That's a big hell, yes.

"Yeah," I grunt out, head already spinning dizzily at the mere idea.

His tentacle gets impossibly thinner. He dips the narrow, slime coated tip inside of my cock, fucking into me in a way I've never gotten fucked before.

"Oh, shit!" I cry out.

I try to jackknife up off the bed at the onslaught of entirely novel sensations as Kirby probes the inside of my dick, but his other tentacles constrict around me. The one in my ass rubs soothingly against my prostate, pumping into me until my cock wants to weep from the building pleasure. Only it can't because he's got me plugged tight. So instead, tears leak down my cheeks. I struggle feebly, but all those implacable limbs hold me fast. I might as well try to fight free of iron chains as try to escape his grasp.

"Mm, yes, you *can* take all of me. We'll just need to get creative, won't we, my mate?"

"Ungh, yeah." I pant as the tentacle in my dick fucks a little deeper, and somehow thickens, like pushing a bead through a straw. The stretch is the strangest thing I've ever experienced. Everything in me squirms at the alien sensation.

I notice a growing fullness and the oddest tickle deep in my groin, like I'm being filled up with more of his slime, fore and aft. Shit, is he really doing what I think he's doing? It hardly seems possible, but his tentacle thrusts deeper with a wet squelch inside of my cock again and I'm almost certain he's getting off.

"Oh my god, is your tentacle coming in my dick?" I demand, caught between horrified awe and wonder that he can make me feel so thoroughly invaded.

"Hush, it needs to be nice and slick." Kirby says, the tickly sensation of fullness not abating in the slightest. "I do not wish to damage you."

Well, that's good. I don't want to contemplate what that kind of damage would entail. Another horrific possibility occurs to me and it takes every ounce of my self control not to flail in his iron grip on my body.

"Swear to god, you better not be laying weird alien eggs inside my bladder, Kirby."

Kirby guffaws, the tentacle in my dick withdrawing slightly and thinning again, as if he wants to take care not to hurt me with his body-shaking amusement. The extra care calms something in me. Whatever this is, to him I'm a treasured mate and so far he's proving to be a fantastic lover, in bed at least. It is utterly outside the realm of possibility to let this go on for long. But I'd be foolish not to take full advantage of the sex god in my bed offering me fantasies I never believed could exist in the real world.

"Are you so eager for young, my mate? I've already told you we cannot spawn unaided. If you wish to copulate in earnest, we can discuss our options later, when I'm not desperate to be inside of you." He wriggles a second tentacle along my rim, pressing it into my ass, slick alongside the first one. That first limb still periodically pulses into just the right spot to keep me panting for more.

"Mm, that's good." It's almost good enough to make me forget my fears, but then the appendage that's sounding my cock slips a little deeper, and fear rushes back to the surface.

What the hell am I doing? This is supposed to be a hot fling, but he's talking about babies. Because of course he is; in his mind, we're newlyweds. I shudder with a visceral revulsion at the mental image of tiny, tentacled babies growing inside of me. No thank you, I am not ready to be a parent with a guy I just met.

Kirby's tentacle pulses thicker against my prostate, reminding me that this is my chance to live out my wildest tentacle fantasies. I can still let him down gently afterward.

"So long as what you're doing to me doesn't mean I'll be stuck birthing them out of my dick, we can discuss kids later," I concede.

I can't even imagine what sort of tentacled horror baby I might have with Kirby. A baby the world can't know about? It seems too dangerous. Besides, a family has never been in my plans. Mostly because I can barely wrap my head around finding a compatible partner in my hazy imaginings of an ideal future. Let alone the other trappings of a stereotypical family life. And honestly, right now, with his tentacles inside me, all I want to focus on is enjoying getting off with my tentacle monster.

"I assure you that an accidental pregnancy is not a possibility. This isn't even my breeding arm." Kirby wriggles a stiffer ninth appendage against my ass. The tip of that one is more blunted than the elegant taper of the others.

I'm pretty sure I'm counting nine limbs wrapped around me and invading my body, anyway. If I'm counting correctly, he has one more appendage than an octopus—not that I've spent ages looking into actual tentacle anatomy when reading up about my alien fantasies. It's not like I can control where my special interests lead me. Regardless, it's heavenly to be bound and at his mercy, as if he plucked this moment straight from my dreams.

"This is going in your other hole. And again, we can't spawn without magical intervention. And the elders' blessing, so you have nothing to worry about."

That's a relief. There's even a small part of me that is flattered he'd actually consider me co-parent material. It's a heady thing to be wanted this intensely. Not only for a night, but for a lifetime. What would it be like if I could have this for real?

I shake the thought out of my head. Our night together will have to be enough to sate all of my desires, and I want to make the most of these memories.

"Okay then. Damn, yes! More." It's too good to deny myself for a moment longer. I'm all in.

It's possible that when the sex haze wears off, I'll question why I fully trust the sea monster with no less than three appendages fucking various parts of me to tell the truth. But the fact remains, I *do* trust him. And I want to ride him. Too bad Kirby is so impossibly strong that I can only squeeze him a little by tensing my ass. He responds by fucking me more slowly and I could cry at the loss of pleasure, so I stop trying to move and let him control this.

"That's it, darling, let me in. Let me take all of you."

"Mm, please, Kirby, need you. Fuck me. The way I like." Will he understand what I mean? He already admitted to spying on my alone time, but does he understand?

"Of course." A loop of slick tentacle slaps against my cheek, then moves in a caress. "Now, be a good little slut and take my tentacles." The admonishment is a little clumsy, like it's his first time playing at humiliation kink. It still sounds so good for him to call me that. Not a generic narrator reading the words of a preset script, but my lover tapping into my deepest core.

"You like that? Being a slut for me?" Kirby repeats the word with more gusto. Fuck, yes, I like it.

I groan at his deep, echoing voice. My own personal sea monster, who wants me to be his good little slut. It's so much better than any fantasy I've ever had.

Kirby *understands* me. He knows how I want to be helpless and at his mercy, while still keeping me safe.

The kraken undulates, and the two limbs pinning my arms to my body tighten and lengthen enough that their tips can stroke along my lips. He teases entry, painting me in his briny musk. "Taste how much you turn me on, mate." Kirby presses into my mouth and I open to him, sucking all the more greedily because he's otherwise got me entirely immobilized with several loops of his tentacles.

The two in my ass pulse, and thin. I whimper at the loss of pressure, but then another one slides in next to the others. It's different from his tentacles, bulging in distinct places as it slithers inside of me.

"Kirby, is that...?"

He's panting, moaning into my neck as he seats himself inside me. "That's my breeding arm. I could put my sperm pouch in there—" He punctuates his words with another greedy thrust, "—and breed your greedy hole."

I whimper at the thought. It might be pretend—thank fuck it's pretend—but it seems so possible. My sea monster needing me, breeding me.

"I'd make you take them all," he tells me. "Fill you up with my babies until you're full."

And, oh, the stretch is incredible, the way he's writhing inside of me, fucking his dick in alongside all those suckers. I feel so deliciously used and debased as he takes my mouth too, a third tip pushing in as the first two hold my mouth open for him. The tentacle invading my mouth is so thick and salty, filling me and pressing at the back of my throat, demanding I suck him like the thickest porn cock.

I have a moment of blind panic that he'll choke me in earnest. He's a creature of the deep; does he have any idea how long a human can hold their breath? I'll choke on his tentacle and he won't even realize he's hurting me. I gasp, gagging on him, desperate to warn him of the danger before it's too late. He pulls back, forestalling my panic. The loop of his tentacle on one of my wrists shifts.

"Make a fist and squeeze," Kirby says.

I don't understand the command, but when he presses a sucker into the center of my palm, I curl my fingers into a fist around it, clinging to him.

"Good boy. If it's too much for my little slut to handle, let go and I'll stop. Understand?" Kirby's beak is so close to my ear, his voice a buzzing purr that soothes away the last vestiges of fear. And damn if his dirty talk doesn't seem totally natural now. He's considered everything, and he's going to take such good care of me. How can I do anything but nod and let him set me adrift in a sea of pleasure?

He pulls out of my mouth enough for me to respond.

"Yes. I'm your slut to use." I get caught up in the moment, desperate for all he has to offer. "Fuck me, Kirby. Mate."

Kirby chuckles, and the vibrations pour through my entire body. I could get so used to sex this amazing being a part of my life. Kirby is going to ruin me for all other lovers if I'm not careful. And then he is fucking my throat, and my ass, and the limb lodged inside my dick eases me open again.

I lose all track of time and place and it's like I'm floating in the ocean, waves of pleasure big enough to drown me swamp my body. Kirby expertly buoys me through it all. He fucks me like he was made to be a part of me. As if we were always meant to come together like this, every part of him filling and fucking every part of me.

Kirby's thrusts are as inevitable as the tides, and I'm as powerless as the beach to take the pounding he's giving me. Laid bare and at his mercy. It's freeing. This is bliss. The pinnacle of sexual experience to be turned inside out with pleasure by a lover who seems intent on reading every muscle twitch. Kirby gives me exactly what I need to stay one touch away from coming.

I choke on his cock-like appendage until stars spangle my vision. He pulls back to let me gasp in a lungful of air at the last moment before I'm certain I need to release his tentacle to beg for breath. My lungs fill and I have time to gasp his name before he thrusts ruthlessly back in, murmuring praises.

"Such a good boy. You take me so good. Such a shameless slut for your mate."

He drives me to the brink again. And again. Until I'm senseless with need and sobbing incoherent pleas for release every time he gives me a breath.

Kirby is the tide. He is the full might of the ocean, and as much as he's making me his plaything, every bit of that power is bent on giving me pleasure. He hums more of that delicious whale song. The tentacle that's been gently probing my dick delves deeper. And I discover my prostate is right fucking there as the vibrations hit it from both sides. I can't hold back any longer.

I writhe violently in his hold as my balls empty and my dick jerks. Kirby pulls out enough to let my cum geyser up out of the tip. His suckers fasten along my length and suckle me through the aftershocks even as his breeding arm pulses deep inside of my ass. The warm rush of more of his slick mixes with a muskier ocean breeze scent, clean and briny.

Ah. So more than slime comes out when he comes. Good to know. Damn, my head is all floaty. Like I've inhaled nitrous oxide at the dentist's office. Giddy and euphoric.

Only this time, the high is natural and I want to float away on it and never come back down. My mate cradles me close and gently withdraws from my body. I whine a protest. He belongs inside of me, buried as deep as possible in my every opening. But Kirby pulls out and his tentacles spread our combined slick over me, making us both smell of sex and the sea. Marking me with the evidence that I am his shameless slut of a mate.

I lay still, caught up in the afterglow. This is glorious—far too wonderful to be my new reality. There has to be a catch. I can figure out what that is when my brain is a little less foggy from probably the best sex of anyone's life.

CHAPTER 7

Release the Kraken

After our second round of amazing sex, we clean up together as best we can with the box of tissues on my side table. I stretch and yawn, savoring all my delicious post-sex aches. The sucker marks on my wrists and elsewhere practically glow with a pleasantly tender warmth.

"Mm. Need coffee," I mutter.

"I should clean my mess from last night. I was excited to introduce myself at last," Kirby offers. Right, I almost forgot about the slime trail he left across my floors. Someone will certainly need to clean that.

I give him a skeptical look. Last I checked, he's the one who covered my entire house with slime, so how is he going to remove it without leaving another trail behind him? I'm still too dreamy and floaty to contemplate it very hard. If he says he wants to mop my floors—if he, in fact, even knows what a mop is—I'm gonna let him do it. It still can't hurt to ask some questions first though.

"Won't that make more slime?"

Kirby chortles, but he ducks two tentacles in front of his face, like he's embarrassed. Odd.

"Um. The slime is a mating response. I only make enough to keep my skin moist on land most of the time. Not enough to leave a mess unless... do you know how many times I came close to greeting you and left before you saw me? You are such a very pretty and intimidating mate."

"Oh." It takes a moment for the penny to drop and I glance over at the clothing he stripped off of me last night. It's stiff from dried kraken pre-cum. Damn. Note to self, kraken lovers are very messy. And that probably confirms he really was my imaginary voyeur the other night. I can't wrap my head around all the implications. "Um, wow. I'm flattered."

We definitely need to talk about all of this. Except right now I need coffee. Lots of coffee. Because I suspect I still might exist in the real world where I need to head into work pretty soon. Though even that sounds surreal right now. I direct Kirby to the bathroom for cleaning supplies. Once he's situated, I make my way to the kitchen to set the heavenly brew to percolate on autopilot, listening to Kirby moving around in the other room.

He comes out to join me as the earthy aroma of the coffee mingles with the tang of the ocean and the lingering scent of sex on my skin. He has my Swiffer spraying the way in front of him. The big fluffy towel from my bathroom is stretched between two tentacles to scrub at the more resistant messy patches. Good to know sex isn't the only time he can put his many tentacles to use.

At the sight of Kirby ambling down my hallway with his utterly inhuman gait, the endorphins fade. That's when I have to come face-to-face with the undeniable reality that I took an actual mythical kraken to my bed.

I look at him—truly look at him for the first time in the light of day. In the darkness of my bedroom, wrapped in the sensuality of living out my deepest buried fantasies, this seemed less overwhelming. In my bright, cheery kitchen, his alienness is plain to see. A massive invertebrate creature manipulating cleaning supplies, I can't get past the fact Kirby has more in common with an octopus than a human.

Sure, he seems to possess all the intelligence of a human, and based on his interpretation of our mating, krakens have a fully developed society and culture all their own. He apparently even knows how to clean ocean slime off a floor. That's more than some of my past boyfriends can claim.

But I had sex with him and he clearly isn't human; the taboo nature of anything that happens between us hits me squarely in the chest like a blow. I might be sick with revulsion at the thought of violating some poor defenseless animal.

Kirby reaches one thick limb toward me, offering a comfort I can't possibly deserve from him. I let him caress my arm anyway, savoring what might be the last time I get to experience the wonderful way his suckers drag over my skin. When he brushes the spots he suctioned onto when he climaxed, there is a tender ache, like a love-bite. Each round little not-quite-bruise is a reminder of what we shared. Of how good it felt to be under his power. To be naked and adored by a force of nature.

"We can't do this. I can't be your mate." I shake my head. As if I can shake the fantasies of a future full of being dominated and fucked by him right out of my mind. I can't, but it's equally impossible to reconcile a normal human life with a sea monster by my side as my lover.

"What do you mean, Tris? It is already done, by the customs and laws of my people. The offering was made and accepted. We have—what is the human term? Made the consommé? Consumed the mating?"

"Consummated," I correct him numbly. This conversation is too surreal. I can't be mated to a kraken. Or mated perhaps, but certainly not married by human standards. "And that doesn't change the fact that you aren't human."

Kirby curls his tentacles in tight, withdrawing the gentle stroking along my bare arm that was anchoring me to the reality of the situation more than I care to admit. I already miss his touch.

"I do not understand. You seemed to welcome our coupling." Kirby's crest wilts and his strange swirling eyes dart around the room, settling anywhere but my face. Like the idea of forcing me is as abhorrent to him as its inverse is to me and he is desperate to escape even the implication.

"I did," I assure him. "That's not the problem."

"Then what is?" Kirby's plaintive expression might break my resolve.

I swallow hard, not wanting to make him think he forced me, but trying to avoid encouraging him either. "It's not about the sex, that was…"

I struggle to find the right word. It was phenomenal. Enough to ruin me for any human lover forever. But if a mating is anything like a marriage, ours is doomed from the start. I shouldn't give him false hope. I don't know a thing about him. Hell, I'm not even sure how long he can survive on the shore.

"Good?" Kirby asks, crest plumping with something that I can only interpret as hope.

"The best." I nod.

I can't bring myself to deny how much I want Kirby, but this is still an impossible dream. Better to send him back to the sea and annul whatever binding he insists exists between us before either of us gets attached. Well, any *more* attached. How is it possible that I already sort of adore the big blob of tentacles gazing up at me after one night in his embrace? I do though. That first blush of infatuation that comes with any new relationship.

"In that case, why would you wish to stop? This is not how things are done in the sea." Kirby curls two tentacles together in front of him. The gesture gives the impression of crossed arms and a pout at the ridiculousness of humans.

"Okay." I pinch the bridge of my nose, unsure how to explain this to him. "I understand your world has different rules than human society, but you say you've watched human media, right? Not only listening in on my, uh, books?"

"Yes. Humans have strange customs. But surely our love can find a way?"

I hold back a chuckle at the cheesy line. It's on the tip of my tongue to tell him you can't fall in love in a night, but damn. I don't want to crush the earnest caring on his inhuman face.

"That is one way of looking at things," I concede. This isn't going the way I'd hoped, and I'm not sure how to get back on the 'we need to break up after the best sex of my life' track. It might be so hard to verbalize, because I don't want to actually say it, as much as the logical side of me knows I should.

"It is a good way, yes." Kirby bobs his big wobbly head. He fixes me with a pleading, hopeful look in those massive alien eyes.

It's all but impossible to resist his charms. And, yeah, as strange as it is to admit, I could see myself falling in love with the kraken in my kitchen. Even the chance for another taste of his tentacles tempts me beyond belief. My resolve waivers, but this can't last. It's simply too good to be true. A fantasy come to life is impossible to trust in.

"I can't be here right now. We both need time apart to think things through. You should go for now, and when I get back from work later, we can discuss how to annul our mating so you're free to pursue a more appropriate mate."

"Annul? What is that? Is it like how we copulated?" Kirby jerks a wandering tentacle back toward his center of mass before it can quite reach my ass.

"Not anal—annul; it means ending whatever mystical bond is influencing you to be with me. I can't begin to predict if this can work out, Kirby. You have been honest with me about your intentions, but I'm not sure if I can do this. No one would understand, and I don't know if I can live a life in the closet."

A tiny voice at the back of my mind scoffs at the excuse. As if I'm really that concerned about holding hands with a man in public, or going on dates to places I hate anyway? I'm turning down my ideal lover over some misguided notion of what love should look like to outsiders? Really?

But he isn't human. Kirby will never be able to pose for the cute framed couples pictures I've envied on my co-workers' workstations. I drop my face into my hands at how shallow that seems, but it's about so much more than the photo. It's about being allowed to live my life openly. That will never be an option with Kirby, and my right to have a picture of my husband on my desk was so hard-won; it's strange to even consider forfeiting it over a sea monster.

"This is not how things work under the waves. If two consenting creatures wish to copulate or become mates, then it isn't for anyone else to interfere. But I will ask the sea sorceresses if they have a solution for us to break the binding, if that is your wish."

"Thank you."

"Of course. You're my mate; I will give you as much space as you need." Kirby's tentacles ripple toward me for a moment. He pulls them back, turns and slouches out the nearest window. He heads toward the sea whence he came. I spend a long time staring after him. Regret and loss mingling and making my stomach sour.

I don't want breakfast or even the coffee I brewed before Kirby came out of the bedroom to join me. Despite the sick roiling in my stomach at hurting Kirby, I still reach to pour a mug. I have a work shift that I need to get ready for, heartbreak or no.

The ring of sucker marks circling my wrist like a bangle has my eyes burning with tears when I catch a glimpse of it as I pour. I don't want this to be my only time with Kirby. I don't want to throw him back when he might be the perfect catch.

Sighing, I wrap my fingers around the tender marks and squeeze, to remind myself that he was real. And I call the one person who might understand. I might not be able to tell the world about Kirby, but Hoyt will listen without trying to get me admitted for a psych eval. He has to believe me, because I'm not entirely certain I believe the last several hours happened myself.

I head back to the bedroom to shower and get dressed. Turns out, the dried crust from last night's Slip 'N Slide through my house isn't just any generic sea monster slime, I'm covered in what amounts to kraken jizz. When I step into the room, I can't help but notice that he not only mopped the floor, Kirby stripped the sex-soaked sheets from my bed too. He might just be a keeper, if only he wasn't aquatic.

CHAPTER 8

He's a ten-tacle, but he's a terror from the deep

"So, let me get this straight." Hoyt fixes me with his most judgmental gaze as he summarizes my distraught rambling. "You spent your precious sleeping time screwing, woke up and fucked him again, and then told him you want a divorce? What the hell, Tris!"

Hoyt gestures at me so emphatically his coffee sloshes onto his hand and he pauses to slurp up the spill. We're sitting in the back of his old sedan in front of our favorite little coffee shop in town. I got the coffee to go since I didn't really want to spill my guts about having said guts rearranged by a sea monster in a public venue.

"What? Did you miss the part where he's a literal sea monster? It's not like we can have a future together." I raise my voice to match his intensity. I don't bother trying to counter his point about my schedule being sacrosanct. Hoyt is well aware of how much unexpected schedule changes throw me. That might explain why I'm cranky this morning. Hoyt meets my energy and raises it another notch.

"Why the hell not? You live next to the ocean on a private stretch of beach. Who is going to know?" He gestures out the window, at the sandy stretch of beachfront behind the quaint little businesses that line Main Street. In the summer months, the rare stretch of sand is always crawling with tourists. Most of our coastline is rocky. Now only a few evening joggers are out braving the chill fall breeze off the waves.

"That's my point!" I wail. And then I continue more calmly. "I want a husband who can come grocery shopping with me. Or keep me company at the hospital holiday party. Someone who I can go on vacations with and introduce to people."

"You can introduce him to me." Hoyt points out with an equanimity I can't match when I am still internally freaking out at the revelations of the past day. Krakens—along with who the fuck knows what other monsters—are real and I let one fuck me. I don't feel like being reasonable. I'm grumpy because I just had the best sex of my life—hell, it was quite possibly the best sex of anyone's life—and I can't keep seeing the man responsible.

Sea beast. He's a mythical sea monster, and I can't actually be married to him. That's just... impossible.

Hoyt rolls his eyes at me. "Dude, be real. You don't enjoy being around people other than me ninety percent of the time. You purposely took a job that means you spend your nights in the hospital basement practically alone. And you complain constantly about the only co-worker you have to interact with regularly."

"So? People are stressful." I cross my arms over my chest. Brad isn't so bad. I guess. If I have to spend time with other people.

Hoyt nods. "That's my point. If Kirby makes you happy, why would you give him up for some hypothetical socially acceptable boyfriend who keeps you company doing things you hate? How does that make sense, when you could be with someone a little less conventional who doesn't expect those things of you?"

I drop my face into my hands and groan, adding several syllables to his name. "Hooooyyyyt, you aren't helping."

"Oh? Was I supposed to tell you to throw him back like yesterday's catch of the day?"

I spread my fingers to glare at him. "Kirby isn't a fish."

Hoyt snorts. "No, more like calamari."

"Shut up! You aren't eating him. He isn't food. He's intelligent and sweet and..." so fucking sexily dominant in bed, just taking me apart like he has the roadmap to my deepest desires. But he made me feel safe while he did it. Cared for. I drag my fingers through my hair, tugging at the roots in two giant fistfuls.

"And you enjoy drinking up all his fish sauce?" Hoyt teases. "Want him to pour it all over you?"

"No! Don't be ridiculous. I just had a delightful night with a guy I probably shouldn't see again. He's so...I don't even know, but that doesn't mean you should go getting ideas about sampling his—uh—fish sauce."

"Uh huh." Hoyt cuts his eyes pointedly to the sucker marks circling my wrists as I rub at them again, to remind myself that Kirby really is real. That's going to be my new go to stim if I don't watch the habit, but I can't bring myself to stop. The tender ache of my fingers pressing where he held me is soothing in a way I can't fully articulate. Lucky for me, I don't have to. Hoyt's teasing grin softens into a genuine smile.

Fuck. I'm pretty sure Kirby has officially ruined me for all other men—or monsters, whatever. The truth is, I loved every second of getting fucked by my sea monster lover and I'd totally do it again. Right now if he emerged onto the shore and my ass wasn't already sore from getting the pounding of a lifetime twice in the past twelve hours.

"First, aw, look at you all tongue-tied over a guy. Second, I would never; I doubt kraken is kosher. Not that I think that would keep him out of *your* mouth." Hoyt winks at me. "As my bubbe would say, you have been poissoned."

"Don't you mean poisoned?" I give him a skeptical look. I suspect if the kraken fluids Kirby pumped into me in the throes of passion were going to make me sick, I'd probably have had a reaction by now. If anything, I feel better than I have in ages. More well-rested than when I first woke up and my usual aches from working hunched at a desk for ten hours a day are almost unnoticeable.

"Nope, poissoned. French for fish." Hoyt cackles when I roll my eyes. I should have seen that coming. It's not the first time he's used that joke. Every time we get sushi he trots it out, and every time I forget about his very limited French vocabulary, picked up from his Quebecois grandmother.

Hoyt is giving me a knowing smirk now. Like he can tell just how thoroughly I've tasted Kirby. And that I loved it. Surely the sex can't always be that good.

Except, it wasn't just that Kirby filled me to my limits and took control in a way that made it easy to let go and enjoy the moment. No. Kirby took care of me. He gave me what I needed before I even realized I needed it. From the ways he touched me to the ways he made sure I could tell him *no*, no matter what.

"Ugh. Is it sad that the most unbelievable part of fucking a ship-destroying kraken isn't his tentacles, it's that he treated me like...I can't even put it into words. He was just respectful while he fucked me like the needy slut I am." The fact that's exactly what I'd want in a perfect partner isn't news to Hoyt.

Hoyt knows all about my struggles to find a guy who will degrade me in bed and make me feel like his treasure the rest of the time. And somehow Kirby strikes just the right balance between doing both at once. His precious little slut, writhing on all nine of his appendages in an ecstasy too overwhelming for any mere mortal.

Hoyt bursts into knee-slapping laughter. I pout at him.

"He's a mensch," Hoyt teases me. "I realize they seem like mythical creatures, but they really *do* exist. Guess you finally kissed enough schmucks to find the one."

"Hardy, har." I scowl at him, and then it hits me that Hoyt has known cryptids are real all along and that means—holy crap. It means he's almost definitely banged them and held out on the juicy details. "Wait—does this mean you've actually had monster sex before?"

"A gentleman doesn't kiss and tell." Hoyt winks at me. The enigmatic schtick would work better if I didn't know damn well he most certainly does tell me just about everything.

"Pshaw, good thing you're no gentleman. Was it that big hairy gym bro with the incredible tongue?" I accuse. Hoyt's lips twitch into a swoony smile.

"Mm, I miss that tongue. Too bad it said stupid things when he wasn't putting it to better uses."

"Oh, yeah. So was he some sort of dual-dicked lizard man?" Another thought occurs to me, and I might owe Brad an apology for his wild theories. There really could be werewolves in Bellweather. "Cory with the silver allergy. Was he one of them too?"

Hoyt gives me a bemused shake of his head. "Swapping sexploits and kvetching about exes with you is one thing, but I don't make a habit of outing cryptids."

"Did your bubbe call or something? You are being particularly Jewish today with all the Yiddish. And if this is one of those times when you go on a 'good Jew' kick, I want some of your challah."

"No. Although my sister is bringing the kids to visit for Sukkot. Apparently, I need to see them more so they can bond with their uncle or something." He waves his hand dismissively, but he's smiling as he talks about his family. "But if you want my baking, bring your mensch to my place for Shabbas dinner some time. I can have a whole spread on. Text me what he eats? Or any dietary restrictions he has."

I grimace. Another thing I don't know about my accidental mate. I'd sort of been assuming Kirby would just eat fish, but I can't really picture him sitting in Hoyt's dining room with the warm glow of candles lighting our meal. This is why I panicked. How can I do normal things, like attending a dinner party with my closest friend and my new partner when Kirby isn't human?

He's not even the sort of cryptid Hoyt has told me about that could reasonably pass as human. You can't put a kraken in a trench coat and a wig and pretend. Can you? No, of course not. He's got a beak, for fuck's sake. A beak and swirling eyes the size of saucers. Not to mention that glorious crest on his head that makes him keen with whale song when he lets me touch it... I am so gone on my mate that it's ridiculous. Perhaps his slime really is an intoxicant because I've never fallen this hard for a guy before. Certainly not this fast.

"Damn, the tentacle dick must be amazing. I've totally lost you to daydreams about your new guy, haven't I?" Hoyt teases me.

"He's... something special. I don't know how I'm going to let him go."

"So, maybe don't? I realize you're new to the whole 'cryptids are real' experience, but you're far from the first person to fall for a monster."

"He's not a monster. I think that's what's tripping me up. He isn't human, but he isn't bad..."

"Most of them aren't. Why do you think they go to such lengths to stay off mainstream humanity's radar? We're the real monsters, hunting what we don't understand. Hurting them. Or worse."

Something about the way he says that sends a chill down my spine. "What do you mean? Is Kirby in danger? I don't want to put him at risk."

"Oh, I'm sure he can take care of himself. Worst case, he can escape into the waves, right?" Hoyt waves away my concerns, but there's more to this, I can see it in his face.

"Hoyt? What aren't you telling me?"

Hoyt sighs, resigned. "Look, I don't want to throw you in over your head or anything, but yeah you have some things to learn. There are forces out there that would hurt him if they could get their hooks into him. If you decide to be with him, the two of you will need to take precautions. But that doesn't mean you can't make a good life together. The sort of quiet, simple existence you've always wanted."

"You think?"

"I *know*."

"How?" I ask.

Hoyt rolls his eyes. "You've met Lida and her kids, right?"

"What does your sister have to do with anything?" I stare at him in disbelief.

"Shit, man." He rubs at his face and searches the heavens, like he's not sure whether to share what he's about to say. "Look, I never said anything before because you wouldn't have believed me or taken the danger seriously. But if I tell you this, you cannot breathe a word to anyone other than your Kirby, you understand? My family's safety is at stake and Lida would justifiably kill me if the wrong people find out. It could be life or death for her kids; you got me?"

"Yeah. I won't tell a soul." I swallow hard at the thought of my best friend's nieces in danger. He dotes on those kids whenever they visit.

"Well, there's a reason you haven't met her partner."

"I thought her ex was a schmuck who ran off and left her when the twins were born."

"That's the cover story." Hoyt nods. "In truth, the kids are half wood nymph. Their other mom is a dryad who can't stray too far from her tree without getting sick, so she mostly stays home when they come to visit."

"You have a secret sister-in-law?" I'm not sure why that's the part I get hung up on, but it is. Lida is in a relationship with a cryptid. Just like I am. I swallow hard at that dose of how strange my reality has gotten.

"Yeah. Nya is very shy, but she makes my sister and the girls happy." Hoyt shrugs. "Who am I to judge?"

"And your sister doesn't mind that she can't tell the entire world about their relationship?"

Hoyt shrugs again. "Lida is happy with her family. She and Nya make it work. And it's not like anyone would believe that the kids are half cryptid."

"They really are? Like, they didn't need a donor or something?" My gut roils at the idea of a half-kraken child somehow growing inside me. But Kirby assured me that isn't possible. *Not without help.* Fuck, is it really possible *with* help? I swallow hard.

Hoyt grimaces and wobbles his hand in the air. "It's complicated, and I don't ask too many questions about my sister's sex life. But the way she puts it is that Nya is part plant and plenty of plants produce multiple types of gametes or self-pollinate. Anyway, let's just say the kids are gifted gardeners and leave it at that. Someday they might have the urge to bond with a tree, but if they don't, they'll be perfectly happy in the human world. There are more hybrids out there than you would think."

"Is that what they like to be called?"

Hoyt shrugs. "I can't speak for every interspecies family, but it's what Nya and Lida use."

"Okay. So. Kirby swore he and I can't..."

Hoyt guffaws. "Well, he isn't a plant, is he? You'll have to defer to his expertise on whether you two can procreate. Do you even want kids?"

"No." I shake my head.

Kids have never been in my plans. But if Kirby and Hoyt are telling me the truth, then I might be able to make biological children with my kraken mate. That might change things for me.

If Kirby wants to make a hybrid baby with me...I might not hate that. At some point in the distant future. And holy carp, am I really making future plans in my head that include tentacle babies? What the hell is wrong with me? There absolutely has to be some sort of psychedelic in Kirby's slime. Maybe I'm just tripping balls.

"Really?" Hoyt raises an eyebrow at me. He knows me too well.

"I guess?" I revise my answer. "It's not like I've considered it much. I didn't think it would be an option. Not without a whole lot of hassle I wasn't ready for. But apparently it's not safe to be a cryptid. Would I really want to bring a hybrid baby into the world if they might not be safe?"

"Well, you can take your time to think about it. There's no rush, right?"

"No, I suppose there isn't. He said we would need to seek help from some sea sorceress or something, so I guess there isn't any chance of an oops?"

"See? There you go. Nothing to fret over." Hoyt claps me on the shoulder. "Now, if you are going to be a part of his world, there are probably some things you need to hear. Promise you'll both come to dinner tomorrow? You don't work, right? Or I can bring dinner to your place if he would be more comfortable there?"

Some of the tension I've felt pulling my body tight since I watched Kirby slink back into the sea leaves my shoulders at the suggestion. "My place for now? I'm not sure how we would get to yours."

Hoyt rolls his eyes, giving me his classic know-it-all smile and head shake combo. "I live on an estuary. It might not be fancy beachfront property like yours, but he could probably make the swim. Or, you know, you could drive over with him in the back seat. Cephalopods are pretty good at squishing into small spaces and hiding."

"Hey!" I want to protest that Kirby shouldn't have to hide, but of course I can't drive around with Kirby's tentacles hanging out the passenger window. I might find his beautiful, beaky face compelling, but that doesn't mean it would be safe to put him on full display to anyone we drive past.

Even driving home in the wee hours of the morning, I sometimes see co-workers who recognize me. It would be far too dangerous to risk discovery by driving around openly with my kraken lover at suppertime. It hits me that my best friend is supportive of my boyfriend being technically a mollusk and I'm struck by how lucky I am to have Hoyt in my life.

Heck, if it wasn't for him, I'd never have made that ridiculous blood oath that bound Kirby to me. I should probably blame him for this entire situation, but it's hard to be mad when I'm still floating on the endorphin rush. I rub my wrist again, another flush of remembered pleasure thrilling through me.

"Right, well, if you're done having an existential crisis, can I congratulate you on the mating?" Hoyt asks.

"You can. I'm not sure it's going to last, but I...might want to see what happens?"

"Good for you. You deserve to be happy, even if that means getting railed by a lord of the deep."

"Mhm." I can't help the mental image of just how deep inside me Kirby was last night. I am so ready to see where this thing with my kraken goes. "Don't be jealous," I tease. And there's a flash of emotion that makes me wonder if he might actually be a little jealous. I must be seeing things. Still, better not rub it in that I've got someone when Hoyt has been struggling with terrible matches on no less than a dozen dating apps for months. "Sorry."

"Don't be." Hoyt waves away my concern. "I really am happy for you. And hey, it can't hurt to ask Kirby if there's another literal fish in the sea for me."

He laughs weakly at his own joke and I join in, but it probably couldn't hurt to ask, right? I mean, Hoyt already knows all about cryptids. And he's told me about how hard it can be to meet people as a trans guy. He's always been so damn earnest about monsters; I wonder how many of his exes are cryptids. In retrospect, I guess I should have listened more to what he was telling me about this stuff. It just all seemed so unbelievable for monsters to be hiding in plain sight in the modern age.

It's fine though, I believe him now. I glance at the time and curse as I realize I need to head to the hospital now. The current pharmacist on duty can't leave until I arrive, so I need to get my butt in gear.

"Got to run, Hoyt, but thanks for listening. I'll ask Kirby about dinner tomorrow. My place at suppertime?" I grab my coffee and phone and reach for his car door.

"Sure." Hoyt nods. "See you then."

"See you, man. Thanks again!" I lift my coffee toward him to encompass the drink and the chat and just being himself. After our talk, I'm daring to consider making this thing with Kirby work. Or at least, I want to give us a chance. If

Kirby still wants that, and if we can make our two worlds collide without too much collateral damage.

As soon as my shift ends, I need to go back to my place and apologize to Kirby for running out on him so abruptly. Hopefully, he won't be too upset. I'm not sure how I'll get in touch with him if he takes my rejection too much to heart and doesn't come back to me in the morning. I wince, recalling the words I flung at him. It will be fine. It has to be. But first, I need to get through work.

CHAPTER 9

Seas the day

I'm tempted to call out sick from work after my chat with Hoyt. It would be a crappy move to leave everyone scrambling for a replacement at the last minute. You can't just close the hospital pharmacy. I mean, with the machines nicely stocked, even in the ER, and the on-call service for emergency coverage, you *can*. But not over relationship drama that I can't explain to anyone at work.

I need to actually have a conversation with Kirby instead of the way I left things with him, but that can wait until after my shift. I was scared of what it might mean to really give this mating thing a chance, but what if it really can work out for us? It's just as well I have a shift. I need time to wrap my head around what that might look like before we talk.

Over the years, I've had to learn to block out my personal life while I'm at work. I push Kirby and the way I left things to the back of my mind to percolate and hunker down in the pharmacy. The animal attack victim we admitted last night still needs IV antibiotics, just to be on the safe side.

"Hey, Doc. Did you see Mr. Allen has already improved enough to be out of the ICU?" Brad asks as he grabs the IV bag to deliver. I verify the vancomycin dosing based on Mr. Allen's evening labs.

"How many times have I told you that you can just call me Tris, Brad?" I roll my eyes at Brad. None of the pharmacists I work with actually use the doctor title our degrees technically entitle us to. This shouldn't be a surprise to him.

"A couple." Brad shrugs. He waggles his eyebrows at me. "Did you see how fast he's improving? Super wolf healing, right? If you know, you know."

"Our patient is not a wolf, Bradley." I resist the urge to rub my temples. Hoyt might be right that I'd complain about any co-worker with the audacity to interrupt my concentration, but Brad pushes my buttons without trying. This college boy is so damn talkative he could chat a rock's ears off.

"Sure, Tris. Whatever you say." Brad winks at me, a suggestive twinkle in his eyes.

Brad's jokes about werewolf bites hit differently now that I've had to accept they're a real possibility. I have to wonder if he actually knows what he's talking about. Does the knowing way his eyes drag over the line of hickies Kirby's tentacle suckers left on my neck, barely peeking above the lapels of my white lab coat just mean he knows I got laid? Or is there a deeper understanding of how they ended up so perfectly symmetrical?

Ugh, I am overthinking this. Brad scoops up a few more pre-packaged dose packs to refill the automated dispensing machine for the second floor med room. Then he leaves the pharmacy, whistling as he makes his deliveries. I press my fingers to the tender red mark on my neck. The ache reminds me of how much I delighted in having my mate's limbs wrapped around me.

When I got ready for work and got a proper look at the marks he left on me, I probably should have freaked out. Or been disgusted. But no, I liked what I saw as I rushed through a cursory shower so I could get to Hoyt as fast as possible. Not just admired it either, the evidence that my mate had marked practically every inch of my skin where my clothing would cover turned me on. It's a good thing it's cold enough for long sleeves because the matching cuffs of sucker marks around both of my wrists and ankles certainly make a statement.

I fucking loved being held in his thrall. That's something I've long since faced about myself. It's just hard to find someone to trust enough to let him fully immobilize me the way Kirby did with such ease. Mostly, I've been settling for porn and what quick release bondage I can safely practice rigging on my own when the need gets too overwhelming. Which always means that if I wanted to, I could easily let myself loose.

Not so with the tentacles that held me, strong as chains. Fuck, the last thing I need to be doing right now is fantasizing about Kirby's tentacles. Imagining him holding me aloft while he takes his time fucking me in holes I didn't even think could be fucked. The way he felt driving into my dick was like electricity applied straight to my balls.

I *so* don't need to be thinking about that at work. I turn on the radio to a station that does an overnight cryptid and conspiracies program. The host is a local guy who puts his own spin on a similar nationally syndicated program, but with a tighter focus on local cryptids, aliens, and all things paranormal.

Hoyt loves this shit, and we grew up listening to similar programs. He's called in enough times that I'm pretty sure he considers the current host, Orion, a friend. The familiar voice of the broadcaster is soothing white noise to get me through my work shift. Another perk of taking overnights is that I can listen to whatever I want. It's usually a peaceful setup for most of the night, with the occasional stat orders for big emergencies.

"Sweet! The Crypt Keeper is supposed to be doing a segment tonight. You're my favorite overnight buddy, Doc." Brad interrupts my calm as soon as he steps foot back inside the pharmacy.

"Tris." I correct him without looking away from my computer. I frown at the stage name that Hoyt uses for his tours and all his public speaking appearances about cryptids coming out of Brad's mouth.

Hoyt didn't mention an interview. He normally tells me about any speaking engagements like this; I am totally going to give him shit when we talk later. I just saw him and he forgot to mention a big thing like this? How dare he.

"Yeah, right. Tris. Think he'll talk about the wolfman attacks?" Brad is practically bouncing with excitement.

He's like an overgrown puppy. If he wasn't so damn disruptive to my routine with his constant interruptions, he might start growing on me. Like a fungus. I notice that I'm rocking in my seat. The stim isn't really helping get me back on an even keel, but at least Brad doesn't make a big deal about it. He definitely notices, I can see him watching out of the corner of my eye. His foot is tapping under his seat and he keeps clicking his pen. I draw the line at snapping at him over his annoying stims, but I turn up the radio to drown out his fidgeting and keep him quiet for a while.

"For the last time, Brad, there aren't any wolves in Maine." I still don't take my attention off my computer monitor even as I want to roll my eyes at him.

"Not natural ones anyway." Brad nudges my shoulder and winks.

"Do I need to make you inventory the IV room again?" I figure the threat will be effective since he's so excited to listen in on my desktop radio.

"Nope, I'm shutting up now." Brad mimes zipping his lips. Kid hates being alone in the sterile prep room. And he wouldn't be able to hear the radio from inside there. He gets back to his tasks for the night and I get back to mine.

"Our next caller is here to discuss an unusual case from the coast of Bellweather." My ears perk up when the host of the program mentions our town. "I've brought on a local expert in cryptozoology. Hoyt Winchester, the local cryptid-hunter community knows him as The Crypt Keeper. Hoyt, thanks for joining us tonight."

"Always a pleasure, Ori."

"So, our last caller brought up the strange disappearance of Craig Delmare. For those who haven't followed the story, Craig was a local entrepreneur and the son of an actual astronaut. He built a home on a strip of beachfront property just outside of Bellweather, Maine. Tragically, last spring he disappeared and has since been declared dead. As far as anyone can tell, Delmare just walked into the sea one morning and vanished. His home was resold by the bank after his family defaulted on the mortgage. Did I miss anything?"

"That's the short version," Hoyt agrees.

It's strange to hear him on the radio. He puts more effort into talking in a deeper register, but it still sounds tinny over the airwaves and through my crappy old speaker.

"And the longer version?" Orion prompts.

"Craig built his home next to what the locals call Devil's Cove. The beach there is cradled between cliffs, and the water is deceptively calm-looking at high tide. But there are large rocks and a powerful undertow, so it's actually quite a dangerous area that the locals know better than to swim in."

"The usual hazards of the sea?" Orion asks, in a skeptical tone.

"Of course. And the sirens who nest there." I can hear the mischief in Hoyt's voice over the airwaves.

"Sirens?" Orion hits just the right balance between credulous and skeptical to stand in for any listener who is on the fence, but willing to be convinced. I used to shake my head at how clearly the host plays on people's emotions to get them to keep listening. He's adept at instilling that kernel of doubt, that the unreal could truly walk among us. Now I just wonder if Orion is in on the truth.

"Yes. Their songs have been known to lure unwary sailors into accidents, so it's not unreasonable to think that Craig might have met a similar grim fate. The last morning he was alive, his clothes were found on the beach and it appears he walked right into the ocean, never to be seen again. No signs of a struggle."

"I see where you're coming from, but who's to say this wasn't just a tragic case of someone overestimating their abilities. Perhaps Craig simply drowned when the conditions proved more dangerous than he expected?"

I can picture the way Hoyt smiles and shakes his head when he knows something you don't before he even opens his mouth to refute Orion. The host is a good foil for him, and they've built a rapport over the years that Hoyt has been professionally involved in cryptozoology.

"Ah, well, normally there wouldn't be much evidence to differentiate. Not with no witnesses. But the footage from his security camera showed him walking right into the waves, not swimming, just walking in until the water closed over his head. And for another, he left behind a journal."

"And have you seen this footage, or the journal?"

"I don't want to reveal my sources, but yes. I've seen the recording, and the journal entries become progressively stranger after he moved to the house beside Devil's Cove. He wrote of songs that haunted him at all hours when he was near the cove. And dreams of a city beneath the sea. His final entry simply says that he is 'going home.' He penned that note, left the journal open to it on his kitchen table, then stripped naked and walked into the waves."

The interview continues with Orion and Hoyt exchanging stories about the sirens and whether they might have been involved in Craig's almost certain death. It's all speculation I'd have scoffed at as flimsy circumstantial evidence and hearsay just days ago. But now I know Hoyt has to walk a careful line between sharing his interest in cryptids with like-minded folks and protecting actual cryptids from harm and exploitation. In that context, it's fascinating to hear the delicate dance he and Orion engage in, right on the edge of credulity.

Hoyt certainly has Brad captivated until the end of the segment. I'll have to thank my buddy for the peace and quiet that gets me through most of the day shift's backlog. I even catch up on all the med orders that have come in since my shift started. But it is a little surreal watching the kid fanboy all over my bestie, with his expertise in his field and his soothing voice.

Hoyt really has a calm vibe going as he waxes eloquent on his favorite subject for a receptive audience.

"Hey, isn't that your house? The one where the dude died?" Brad asks when the segment goes to a commercial break. I turn down the volume on a discount store jingle and shrug.

"Yep. Got it for a song," I say. Hoyt would punch my shoulder for that joke and accuse me of tempting the fates. I would have dismissed his fears out of hand only yesterday. Now I can't help a smug pride that my mate wouldn't let me drown. Because I somehow have a mate. Life is strange.

Brad's eyes widen with horrified delight. "Do you hear them singing? Did he leave his stuff? OMG! You live near real cryptids, Tris; tell me everything!" He looks like he wants to grab my shoulders and shake answers out of me. I shrink back in my seat and tap my thumb against each fingertip in turn. This kid is so overeager it's exhausting just listening to him. No wonder I have a hard time masking around him.

"Nope, I haven't heard a thing." That would even have been mostly true before yesterday. How in the hell has everything changed so fast? Last night, I'd have scoffed at how gullible Brad is being. And now I've got lines of Kirby's sucker marks banding my torso. I rub surreptitiously through my sleeve at the ones around my wrist.

Brad's eyes dart from the purplish bruise at my neck to my self-soothing gesture. His eyes narrow in thought. "Yeah, I guess you wouldn't be just sitting there if sirens were calling you into the deep, huh?"

"Exactly." I nod. I'm a terrible liar, so I don't even try to deny that such fantastical creatures could exist. "The only singing I've heard is a bunch of noisy seagulls screeching when anything gets too close to their nests."

"You know, that makes sense." Brad nodds.

"How so?"

"A lot of lore acts like sirens are just a more carnivorous version of merfolk, but sometimes they're not fish people at all."

"Oh?"

"Yeah. Some of the old Greek stories my yaya used to tell me say they were part bird. You know, because of the singing." Brad shrugs. "My brother used to joke that his superpower is immunity to sirens."

"Hey, that's mine too."

Brad gives me a skeptical look. "Why?"

"Because I'm not attracted to women."

Brad scoffs. "Man, there have got to be gay sirens. You really are tempting fate, living on their doorstep just because you think only women sing or something? Everyone knows male birds have the more impressive mating displays. Be careful or you'll end up just like that Craig guy."

"I'll keep that in mind."

"Yeah. You should."

I snort. "Why is your brother immune to their charms?"

"Rhys is Deaf, so it's hard to lure him with songs he can't hear. Yaya said it's not actually music you hear with your ears though, so maybe he wouldn't be safe either?" Brad shrugs. "Still, couldn't hurt to sleep with earplugs, right?"

"Right," I say, totally deadpan. After meeting Kirby, I might have to rethink just how seriously I should take all these dire warnings about my siren neighbors. The rumors about their unique take on inviting my home's previous owner over for dinner aren't outside the realm of possibility. Chock that up as another thing I should discuss with Kirby. It's possible he saw what happened to Craig. Or he can find out.

Brad yawns, glancing at the clock. "I'm going to grab a coffee. Want anything from the cafe, Tris?"

"I'll take a refill on my coffee. Two creamers, please." I nudge my reusable mug toward him and pull out a couple of bucks to cover the cost for both our drinks. "If I realized telling you I have monsters in my backyard would get you to actually use my name, I'd have said something sooner. Grab our caffeine fix and then get back to work, kid."

Brad grabs my mug, pockets the cash, and salutes cheekily. "Be right back with the goods, Doc."

So much for getting him to use my name, but the kid's beaming smile sparkles with amusement as he says it, so I don't rise to the bait. I find myself smiling at his antics as the pharmacy door shuts, cutting off his cheery whistling. The kid might not be so bad. And if he's this into cryptids, maybe it wouldn't hurt to befriend my scatter-brained co-worker.

CHAPTER 10

Making it of-fish-ial

I 'm not sure what to expect when I get home. My house doesn't look any different than usual. That shouldn't come as a surprise. It's just that with the way my entire view of the world shifted yesterday, it's surreal for everything to look the same as it ever has. I pull into my driveway, park, and take a moment sitting there to collect myself.

I can see from the car that the door into the mudroom is shut. That should mean a better start to my day already. So why does it make my heart sink that when I actually go inside, there isn't a horny sea creature's slime trail greeting me at my front door?

"Kirby?" I look for him as I hang up my keys and take off my shoes. "Are you home?"

Silence.

I call for him a few more times as I pad past the kitchen and living room, down the hall to my bedroom. There's no sign of him anywhere. Unless the mess we made of my sheets counts. It still smells like sex on a beach in here, but the sheets are bundled up where Kirby left them after removing them from the bed.

I never got around to showing him the laundry closet in the hallway. Sea brine and sex musk linger in the air, not quite as appealing after congealing into a crusty mess all night long. I sigh at the sheer amount of laundry and set to work. First, I dig out the spare sheets so I can be sure I still have them handy. This way I won't have to wait until the soiled sheets are dry to go to bed once I throw them into the machine.

I set the navy blue and cream striped sheets on the bedside table, then strip the mattress protector off the bed. It could use a wash as well from the sheer amount of—ahem—fish juice that Kirby produces in the throes of passion. Good thing he doesn't make nearly as much slime when he isn't aroused.

I bundle everything down the hall and into the washing machine. There's a crashing sound in the distance as I'm measuring out my laundry soap to start the load.

"Kirby?" I call, wondering if he has returned. But the door hasn't opened and surely I'd have seen him slipping inside?

It was probably just the ocean or something equally innocuous. I add the detergent and set the machine to a bulky item cycle. I'll swap it over after I wake up. It was a long night, and a certain sea monster kept me up half of my usual sleep window yesterday.

The first thing I notice when I step back into my bedroom is the blackout curtain swaying in the breeze from the open window behind it. Odd. I always keep those closed.

Then I hear the low humming buzz of the kraken's whale song. I turn to see him putting his tentacles to good use, stretching the fresh fitted sheet and mattress protector over the entire mattress in one go. He seems to be struggling with how to secure the edges under the mattress.

I stare, jaw on the floor because holy carp, I never thought I would be jealous of a bedsheet of all things. I have a sudden visceral need to be the one splayed spread eagle across a mattress under my mate, utterly at his mercy—just like that stretch of taut fabric.

"Oh, good! You're here." Kirby's crest plumps and he flutters his massive guileless eyes endearingly at me. "Help me get this thing to stay in place? There must be some trick I missed on the shows. It keeps pulling away from the corners."

Chuckling weakly at the sheer surreal domesticity of helping my kraken lover put sheets on my bed, I go to lift the nearest mattress corner for him. Kirby quickly repeats the motions with each of the other sides and soon the bed is covered in the crease-free expanse of fresh linens. Kirby turns to face me with what I'm nearly certain is a smug look. Can a kraken look smug? Well apparently, yes. Who knew?

"How was your night, dear?" Kirby asks, like he's been watching too much *I Love Lucy*.

"You came back," I breathe, staring at him, but not quite believing it.

"I'm sorry? You called for me. I know I promised to give you space, but I thought calling me back meant you'd decided that you wanted me..." Kirby shrinks in on himself. He pulls his tentacles into a tight, miserable ball. As if he could somehow make himself small or unimposing. It's unspeakably endearing and at the same time, I want to kick myself for making him feel unwanted.

"No." I start toward him and Kirby flinches, edging back toward the window. Ah, so I did shut it. He just let himself in that way. "Don't go! I meant I'm glad you came back. I was too hasty and harsh with you before work. I—this isn't something I expected."

"You asked for the mating." Kirby's swirling eyes fix on me, and he puffs up a little, tentacles reaching hopefully toward me. He still sounds hurt and confused.

I rub my temples. "Yes, but I didn't realize what I was doing with that ritual."

Kirby's nictitating membranes slide across his massive eyes twice and his beak clacks. "I'm sorry. Did you just say you did a binding ritual with your own blood without understanding what it was?"

"Um, yes?" I bite my lip and rub anxiously along his marks on my wrist. A potent reminder that it all worked out fine.

When he puts it like that, it sounds unspeakably foolish. But I had no idea cryptids were real, let alone that they could seal magical mate bonds with my blood. I reach toward Kirby and he loops a coiling tentacle over my hand, then around my wrist to climb all the way up my arm in spiraling coils. His touch sets off the tender hickies he left on me earlier. It's a tempting reminder of just why I'm not the least bit sorry I made such a foolish move.

I'm not sorry that he's my mate. I'm just uncertain if I can really commit my life to anyone I only met a day ago. No matter how good the sex might be.

"My mate is very brave. Or very foolish." Kirby pets me with his tentacles, his strange caresses comforting in ways I can't begin to describe.

"We can say brave," I offer. And fuck it, he can smell my arousal, how much his every touch turns me on. There's no point in trying to hide anything from him.

Kirby squeezes my arm and tugs me closer to wrap me in more of his limbs. I let out a breathy moan. I can see the much stubbier and less sinuous breeding arm he fucked me with when we woke up together poking out amongst the others. Surely that means he's still into me too?

Kirby chuckles and wraps around my other arm, urging me toward the bed. "My brave little slut is insatiable. Does that mean you wish to honor our mating? The sea sorceresses can help us break it, if that is still your wish."

"No. I don't want to break our bond. I just...can we try things the human way too?"

Kirby recoils, then cocks his head. "What is this human way you refer to?"

"You've watched movies, right?" I ask.

"Yes, many movies and radio dramas on the big ships and ashore."

"So you're familiar with dating, getting to know each other in a relation-ship?"

"You wish me to woo you with food?" Kirby cocks his head quizzically.

"I mean, I guess?" I shrug, unsure what I'm even asking for. "Dates and stuff."

"Oh." Kirby slumps, the grip on my arm loosening. I hate seeing him so dejected.

"What's wrong?"

"I cannot accompany you among other humans." Kirby waves several of his tentacles, so woebegone, I want to reassure him it doesn't matter. But what if it does?

What if I can't be happy tying myself to a kraken mate and I'm just deluding myself to think otherwise? I can practically hear Hoyt in my head, reminding me that the last time I went on a date, I ended up bailing by the time the appetizers arrived. I took my meal home in a to-go container. The truth of the matter is that I don't want to spend my time among most other humans regardless. So why would not being able to spend my time with Kirby doing things I hate be a deal-breaker?

"I am aware of that. It's why I wasn't sure I could do this with you. But maybe we can find a way to make things work?"

"You are sure?" His tentacles twine over each other. Two of them run up my legs, caressing my thighs, pushing up under my shirt. A sucker fastens over my nipple, making me gasp and arch into his touch. "I wouldn't wish to keep you from your friends and family."

Through the haze of pleasure, I recall something important. "Um, you don't have to. My best friend invited us to dinner tonight. Like a sort of date? Or dinner party? It would just be the three of us."

"Yes? He knows of me? You told him I am a kraken?"

"I did. Hoyt already knew about cryptids. He's the one who told me the words of the ritual. Except I think his information was faulty. It was supposed to protect me from sirens' songs."

Kirby's crest ripples, and he makes an amused sound. "That's just silly. Even a spawnling knows you need to carry a moonstone against your skin to block their songs. Besides, the sirens who live in the cove won't bother a kraken's mate, even if all the land folk here weren't already under my protection. But if you are worried, I can y when he gets here. He's coming over to eat a little after sunset."

Kirby's crest flares larger. "You won't have long to sleep then. The days are short now."

"Yeah. He's worth getting a little less sleep for, and so are you." I pat the tentacle that's still snuggled near my neck. "I need to throw dinner into the slow cooker before we go to bed, actually."

Kirby's touch lingers a moment longer. He steals a kiss before trailing me into the kitchen to observe me chopping veggies and throwing ingredients into the Crock-Pot to simmer.

"There, all we have to do now is wait and it will be delicious at suppertime."

"Perhaps, but not as delicious as you," Kirby says, moving closer.

As soon as I set the timer, he's on me, coaxing me back to bed with gentle but firm touches. Kirby is so affectionate with me. It's strange, but I could get used to this; being touched and treasured and...oh, fuck! He found my dick again and I am *so* beyond okay with being a little tired later, no matter how much any changes in my schedule throw me off. Right now, sex seems more important. The perfect distraction from worrying whether my best friend still approves of this match after meeting an actual kraken in person.

CHAPTER 11

Tenta-cruel to be kind

I wake up to a warm tentacle wrapping around my morning—well, with my schedule, evening, but either way—wood and my mate whispering in my ear.

"It is almost time for your friend to arrive. I wish to mark you first. Is that agreeable?" Kirby makes cute little chirruping sounds.

"Uh? Huh? How?" I reach to rub blearily at my face, but Kirby catches my wrist and holds me fast. "Mm. Have I told you how much I like when you do that?" The words slip out because I'm too sleepy to realize the power I'm granting him by admitting just how hot I find being totally overpowered by him.

"Yes." He makes a clicking sound. "Your scent says as much." Kirby presses his tentacles against my skin, as though he wants to taste every inch of my skin with them. He strokes along my jaw, probing at my lips until I part them. I suckle on his tentacle tip as he pushes into my mouth. Kirby's crest flutters and he makes a pleased cooing sound. "My sweet mate loves to be held at my mercy, don't you?" he burbles.

He wraps his coils around my wrists a few more times, holding me fast as he stretches them above my head.

"Yes," I admit around the probing digit in my mouth.

I'm not even ashamed. There's no room for shame when Kirby is prodding at my hole and playing with my cock. I suck him like the desperate, needy slut he seems to enjoy calling me almost as much as I love to hear those words. The memory of him telling me he likes to spy on human movies flashes through my head.

Kirby admitted to needing time to work up to introducing himself. How many times in the past few weeks that I've lived here has he listened in on my favorite porn? The filthy scripted words the burly Dom tops used for the needy begging sluts flash through my mind. Yeah. Kirby has my number for sure. That should feel like a violation, but Kirby wanting to learn what turns me on only warms me down to my toes.

Kirby stretches my arms to the limits of how far I can comfortably reach, giving another set of his sucker-lined tentacles access to my armpits. When I squirm and make a disgruntled noise at the back of my throat, Kirby's massive eyes light with mischief. He tickles me mercilessly until I gag on the tentacle in my mouth, trying to beg for mercy.

"Oh, yes. You taste divine, mate of mine. I am going to have you. And if you are a very good slut for your mate, then perhaps I will reward you...after your friend leaves." He pulls out of my mouth enough for me to speak, stroking my saliva over my cheeks and lips as he coos his filthy promises.

"No! I'll be so good." I groan, ready to beg him not to tease me. Not to edge me for hours and keep me in a heady state of arousal in front of Hoyt.

"I know you will, my mate. You will be a perfect little cum dumpster for me, holding all my spawn inside of yourself. You'll keep it all inside you until I'm ready to fuck it back out of this tight little hole after dinner, won't you?" Two tentacles tap at my hole and I obediently spread my legs to give him better access.

Oh fuck. Now that he's spelling it out, I kind of do want that. Not for him to pull Hoyt into some sort of sex game without letting him know. I just crave the constant reminder of how good Kirby makes everything between us in bed. The threat of sitting at the table, plugged and full of his seed while we talk, has me all hot and bothered. The only issue with that plan is I'm not sure I'll be able to focus on whatever big serious secrets Hoyt seems to think we should know now that I'm a part of this secret world of his. A world that includes krakens coming out of the sea and—well, coming all over me. Whatever, I'll make it work.

Thinking about my friend when my dick is so hard that it aches is awkward. Kirby takes my mind off the weirdness, tentacles wrapping me up in him, painting me in the slime that becomes plentiful now that he's turned on. I want to be full of his essence, an inescapable reminder nestled inside of me, telling me I belong in a way I never have with any other lover. A promise that I can be a part of his world even as he insinuates himself into mine.

"Yes. I want that. Fuck me, Kirby, make me yours."

Kirby spins me so that my back presses against his center of mass, several appendages probing suggestively at my ass even as he nuzzles his beak behind my ear. The length that had been invading my mouth dives back in and thickens, making further conversation impossible.

"You are already mine." Kirby all but hisses against the shell of my ear. The cool smoothness of his beak is strange against my skin. The vibrations of his words send pleasure thrumming along my nerves. "My perfect slut."

"Mmph!" I can't get enough of his dirty talk. His words fill me with a shivery need to be exactly what he wants. To be stuffed and claimed by my mate. Desire surges hot inside me with his every word and touch.

The tentacle coiled around my dick squeezes in concentric rings that have me stiff as a rod in an instant. Kirby milks me until a fat drop of precum wells up and spills over to slick his stroking. He traces his tentacle tip around my cockhead, dipping in under my foreskin before teasing my slit like he did when he fucked into me there the other night. I whimper, caught between need and a sensation that pushes the boundary between so hot I might ignite and too much to take.

"I'm going to fill you up now. Open for me." He taps at my pucker.

I do my best to spread my thighs even wider for him to press inside. Suckers fasten around my rim, the sensation unlike anything I've ever experienced or even imagined. It's like several mouths have fastened onto the sensitive skin of my rim, sucking and caressing, pushing more of his slime into me to ease his entry. Kirby might just kill me with pleasure.

The tentacle tracing my slit dips inside my cock. Kirby feeds his slime inside to slick the way as he sinks in deep enough to nudge against my prostate. His tentacle sets off more of those delightful sparks from the first time. Damn. The electric intensity of being sounded has me almost out of my mind with need. I suck him harder, desperate to show him how good he's making me feel and unable to do it any other way.

Kirby's tentacles hold me in the bondage from my dreams. A living, breathing constriction that commands my every breath. I can only move if he allows it, no hope of wriggling loose from the restraints so skin-tight they're suctioned into place all over my body. The sense of being completely restrained by him is exquisite. I'm loving every minute of this.

Kirby fucks his tentacle into my mouth, stroking me inside and out. All of my holes are full of him as he holds me in place. He is my entire world as I relax into the unyielding grip on my body. His appendages fuck me in leisurely thrusts, swelling and thinning with every stroke. Every time he fucks into me, it's a whole new experience and I can't get enough of this. Can't get enough of him.

I surrender entirely to my mate, letting him take me, bring me to the brink and back down. He edges me over and over, taking me higher with each ascent toward a pinnacle he's careful to keep just out of reach. It's like swimming in the ocean to allow the waves to toss me back ashore. As if each wave of pleasure tosses me higher before I crash down into the next trough. Then he catches me and throws me to even greater heights and I can't calm my ragged breathing or control a thing. I'm entirely at the mercy of a force of nature stronger than any mere mortal could ever hope to conquer. Lucky for me, I don't want to be the one in control.

Kirby has my prostate practically buzzing from the dual-pronged stimulation. He seems to find it unerringly where he's firmly nestled inside both my ass and my dick, possessing me as no other lover could. All my focus is on him and the way his tentacles fuck me better than I ever imagined possible. Sex with him is incredible.

"Such a good slut for me," Kirby croons, withdrawing from my mouth just enough for me to breathe his name in a keening plea for release.

"Please, Kirby. Need to come," I sob. His words combined with the intense pleasure of having my prostate milked have me teetering on the brink. It's all too much.

Kirby burbles happily. "Not yet. You hold that orgasm for me, mate." He strokes me again, a coil of his tentacle squeezing my balls just tight enough to stave off the pleasure. "Going to fuck my cum into you. Think you can hold it all in for me?"

I nod frantically with the slack he gives me to respond. Kirby purrs and then another appendage, the thick stubby breeding arm, pushes inside. He fucks me with a rigid implacability that his tentacles lack. He pulls out of my mouth enough that I can beg.

"Oh, more. More, Kirby!" I try to writhe in his grasp, relishing in the way his tentacles hold me fast. Kirby pins me in place for him to take his pleasure even as he tests my limits in every way possible.

"If you come, this all stops," Kirby reminds me. I moan my needy assent around the tentacle in my mouth. "Good boy."

Fuck. Those words have my balls drawing up tight. I'm so close, a hair trigger from exploding. It's going to be impossible to hold back, but I want to do it for him. I want to play this game and follow his rules and not worry about anything to do with the outside world.

Kirby splits me open and fucks me hard, taking me right to the brink, more tentacles slipping inside until I lose all track of how many times I'm being penetrated. So many tentacles I can't keep track of them all.

Kirby is fucking me in half a dozen different rhythms, tentacles thrusting and pulsing, slick dripping everywhere. He's a one person orgy, and I'm loving every second. And then I'm cresting the peak. It takes everything in me to hold back as his wet heat fills me right to the brim. He plunges in deep, stuffing me until my belly cramps from the sheer amount of his release and all the thick tentacles stretching me to my limits.

Kirby fucks me through it, shallow thrusts in all my orifices that keep me suspended at the highest of heights, flying for him as I've never done before. It's all too much when he caresses my face and gently withdraws from my ass to stuff me with my biggest plug. Hot tears of need spill down my cheeks. Kirby brushes them away with his suckers.

"Such a beautiful little cum-stuffed morsel."

That's what tips me over the edge, the sweet longing in his voice that shows I'm not the only one utterly enamored. I come, my dick pulsing in his hold and for a moment the sheer bliss is like I truly am flying. Until the hold on my balls tightens to an almost crushing force. Not enough to do damage, but enough to ruin the orgasm in combination with the swift withdrawal of all his other limbs.

Suddenly, I'm adrift and empty. No more tentacle in my mouth, stretching my lips wide so my saliva dribbles uncontrollably along his length to mix with his natural, briny juices. I whimper my distress at the loss of his touch.

No more strong limbs wrapped around me, holding me together. No more powerful grip pinning my arms and legs. Kirby withdraws from me, leaving me bereft. No more gentle probing at my rim where the plug is keeping me full of him. No more caressing my cock, filling and stroking it. I'm left untouched and untethered as I come crashing back to earth.

Mentally and emotionally, it's like a splash of cold water to the face for him to pull away as my cock pulses. My balls pump out jets of cum like something out of a porno. Kirby stands back watching me as I physically come harder than I've ever done in my life. Even as my dick geysers, the pleasure that usually accompanies an orgasm swims beyond my reach because I need him with a feral intensity.

I ache for his touch, for the pleasure and domination that brought me here and then abandoned me at the critical moment. I sob as the ruined orgasm—rendered purely an autonomic response now—wracks almost painfully through my body, disconnected and spinning. Nothing but the vessel he used and discarded.

My dick stops throbbing at some point, my balls empty. My gut still cramps from being overfilled with his cum. I curl around myself in the bed, burying my nose in our combined scents. His sea brine pheromones and the aching reminder inside me; I did that.

I'm the one who made this powerful ruler of the deep lose himself in pleasure. It gives me some solace amidst the crushing defeat of disappointing him. I wasn't supposed to come and now Kirby apparently doesn't want me because I failed him. Yet he stays by my side despite withdrawing his touch.

"Shh, I know, mate. But you didn't have permission. You'll get to enjoy the next one, I promise," Kirby croons soothing sweet nothings as I bite back a whining demand for more.

A sob wracks my body, shaking me as the tears burn tracks down my face. The salty tang of them on my lips only reminds me of my lover and makes me ache for his touch all the more.

The bed creaks, and I imagine Kirby leaving me there, a sobbing wretched wreck. Will he ever return? Is this how he felt when I rejected our mating? Except Kirby doesn't get up or abandon me. Instead of leaving, his warm weight drapes over my back, and then I'm wrapped in his eightfold embrace, his beak nestled by my ear again.

"Such a beautiful boy for me. You are ethereal as the waves crashing against the shore when you come. Offering me an ocean in your eyes." His tentacle tips take my face delicately in their grasp and brush away my tears. "My perfect mate. An ocean all my own to explore. And I will plumb all of your depths. You are mine and I am going to give you such pleasure later, tenfold what you just gave to me," he promises.

I shiver at the intensity behind his words. "Don't go?"

"No, of course not. I'm right here, mate." Kirby holds me until I stop shivering and I'm less jittery from the crash of that ruined orgasm. As punishments in bed go, that might be my least favorite now. But he made it clear I wasn't allowed to come before dinner. "Was that too much for you?"

"No. I don't know if I like that, though."

Kirby nuzzles his smooth beak into my neck. "You aren't meant to enjoy punishments, mate of mine. It will make it all the better when you do have permission to come later. Unless ruining your orgasms is a limit?"

I consider, and then I shake my head. There's a part of me that loves the intensity of the entire experience, the possessive control over my pleasure. "No. I, uh, it was intense. Just need to hear that you're still with me, that you still want me. I don't want to disappoint you."

"You could never disappoint me. And I will always stay by your side when you are so vulnerable for me."

"Good. This is nice."

"It is. But we should get ready now, if you're up for it? I wish to take care of you."

"Yeah. Okay."

"Good mate. Come into your bathing room; we should clean the brine from your skin before it dries. Your friend will arrive soon, yes?"

I glance at the clock and groan. Yeah. Hoyt will be here soon. We don't have much time to get ready. I need to check on the slow cooker chicken soup I put on before getting into bed.

I've got the boxed matzo dumpling batter ready to roll into balls and drop into the pot. There's also a fresh frozen loaf of bread dough I stuck in the fridge before work to defrost and rise. I check on the loaf on the counter, finishing rising as I preheat the oven. That should be an adequate meal, especially if Hoyt brings dessert. I'm hoping for his triple chip cookies, but I'll take anything that man bakes.

It suddenly occurs to me I have no idea if my mate even eats human foods. Will offering him cooked meat bother him?

"Kirby?" I freeze in his embrace and Kirby strokes me tenderly, immediately concerned.

"What is it? Did I hurt you?" Two of his tentacles twine together in front of him, for all the world as though he's a human wringing his hands in worry.

"No. I'm good. Full." My face heats at the admission. I like the sensation and from the proud way his crest puffs up, he knows it. "Can you even eat dinner with us?"

Kirby clacks his beak in amusement. "Oh, yes. I enjoy human food on occasion, though kelp and fish are my preference."

"Ah. We'll have to get sushi for one of our date nights then."

"Yes." Kirby nuzzles into my neck. "I will try all of your human delicacies." Something about the way his tongue flicks against my neck tells me he isn't restricting that plan to the dinner menu. He's a keeper, and I'm in awe of how I landed this charming creature and made him mine.

CHAPTER 12

Catch of the day

I have another armload of dirty sheets to stuff into the washing machine after our shower. Kirby is busy swapping the clean ones onto the mattress now that he has the trick of it down. The sight of him manhandling the mattress like it weighs nothing is scorching hot. Doing it while simultaneously stretching his powerful limbs to secure the fitted sheet over each corner is more than enough to have me aroused all over again. Enough so that I have to excuse myself to check on the food or risk ending up right back in bed.

We don't have time for any more filthy fooling around. The plug in my ass and the lingering ache of a thorough fucking earlier are more than enough of a distraction. The soup simmering away in the slow cooker makes the house smell amazing when I venture out of the bedroom. To my relief, it also masks the musk of sex and the sea that lingers in my room even after stripping the bed.

When I start my load of laundry, the detergent perfumes the air even more. Good. Hoyt doesn't need any ammunition to tease me mercilessly about being all loved up once he arrives.

Thinking of his impending arrival, I need to shape the matzo balls and get them simmering, and then everything should be ready by the time Hoyt arrives. I preheat the oven, then get the balls boiling. By the time I set the timer for the soup, the oven is ready for me to pop the thawed bread dough in to bake. The forty-minute timer for the matzo balls is perfect for the bread as well. It should be perfectly golden and delicious around the time Hoyt arrives.

I fuss over setting the table and tidying the house. Kirby already cleaned up his slime trail from the other night. But now the rest of the floor looks like it needs a good mopping to match the sheen of the pathway he scrubbed for me. Before I know it, I'm caught up in chores until Kirby wraps me in his tentacles and prods at the plug in my hole, reminding me I'm all his.

Kirby clings onto me, latching on from behind like a limpet. He nuzzles into my neck with his beak, reminding me of all the wickedly wonderful things he does to me.

Ugh. Is it too late to cancel on Hoyt and just spend my night off wrapped in my lover's tentacles? Surely we can take a few days to just pretend the outside world doesn't exist?

Except Hoyt told me there were things we needed to know for our safety and he isn't one to exaggerate about something like that. I trust his judgment about whatever is going on. Besides, if the sirens in the bay are as real as my mate, I might need actual protection from them, rather than laughing them off as not my type. Even if Kirby seems confident that our mating should be protection enough.

His tentacles rub me in a tantalizing tease as I finish wiping down the kitchen counters. I'd scold him for getting in the way, but honestly, I like his blatant interest. It's nice to be wrapped up in him. I don't expect that to be how we are forever, but the electric buzz of excitement whenever he pays me attention is nice for now.

Besides, I'm really just making tasks for myself at this point. The laundry is tumbling dry, the kitchen and dining room are spotless and the timer for the food alerts me that dinner is ready. That's when headlights sweep through the evening's gloaming as Hoyt's Subaru pulls into my driveway.

Hoyt honks a little tune, making me smile at his unique way of announcing his presence. The giant dork. I know he's going to make some ridiculous comment about wanting to give us newlyweds plenty of warning. I'd roll my eyes, but he's as endearing as he is infuriating, and I can't stay mad at him.

"He's here." Kirby's tentacles withdraw, balling up under himself in that way that minimizes his size and how intimidating he looks.

Is—is he nervous? I don't like to see him shrink to fit in with humans, and I miss his touch. At the same time, a small part of me is elated that he cares so deeply about making a good impression on my best friend. Like he understands the weight this first meeting might have on the longevity of our relationship.

Kirby's reaction has me getting nervous all over again, fretting about how the next few minutes could go terribly wrong. My face falls.

Kirby lifts one slender limb to pat my cheek. "It's alright. You are mine, no matter what any human thinks. Remember that." Another of his tentacles taps the plug through my pants, nudging it into my prostate and reminding me just how full of Kirby I still am. It would be beyond embarrassing to dislodge the plug and let his fluids dribble into my pants while Hoyt is here. So I clench around the reminder of my mate's claim on my body and nod reluctantly.

"You can't do that while he's here!" I protest, swatting at the tentacle that's reaching behind me.

"Of course not, my mate. But you will remember to whom you belong, yes?" Kirby slides in close to me. His beak nuzzles my wrist where I've been rubbing the sucker marks. He caresses my lips with the tip of one teasing tentacle. I wish he could wrap me up in them again, but that probably wouldn't help me with keeping things PG in front of our guest.

"Yes." My breath hitches. The kraken plays entirely dirty. I am in so far over my head with him, but he makes me feel amazing. That's not something I want to take for granted.

A loud rap to the tune of shave and a haircut sounds from the heavy wood of the front door. "Knock, knock," Hoyt calls in his rich tenor. He sounds amused, and I peer around my mate to see him waving at us through the window on the door.

"Who's there?" I grumble, rolling my eyes, more at myself for being annoyed when we made plans for him to meet Kirby than at the interruption. I rub the embarrassed heat from my cheeks as I step away from Kirby to greet Hoyt.

"Hoyt, but you already knew that. Hello, darling." He smacks an air kiss near my cheek that has Kirby edging between us and Hoyt grinning at the subtle display of possessiveness. "I brought more of that caviar you liked so much last time. Figured your mating merited a celebration, and the big guy might like it."

Hoyt winks as he hands me the fancy little imported tin. He nudges Kirby's closest tentacle in a sort of fist-bump, as if they've been friends for ages, and he hangs around with tentacle monsters daily.

I gape at Hoyt. He's taking the sea creature standing in my doorway much better than I did. And then I flush, thinking about all the ways I've taken Kirby since then. I really don't want to think about Hoyt having a similar level of intimacy with my kraken.

Hoyt gently raps the back of his hand against my abs. Fuck, is it my imagination or does his playful slap make the sea of fluids Kirby left inside me slosh? Imagination or not, it reminds me deliciously of being utterly at my mate's mercy. This is going to be a long night with the ever-present reminder gnawing away at the edge of my awareness. Kirby gives me what I swear is a knowing smirk, though it's hard to be sure, given the beak in place of human lips and wide deceptively innocent eyes.

"Well, aren't you going to introduce me to your man, Tris?" Hoyt demands.

"Oh. Um. Yes. Hoyt Winchester, this is Kirby, Terror of the Deep and Destroyer of Storms."

"You forgot Vanquisher of Tristan's insatiable h—" Kirby interjects.

"Heart! My insatiable heart!" I jump in, narrowing my eyes at Kirby. The sea beast is definitely fucking with me.

"Mhm, yes, your delightful—heart." Kirby's crest ruffles with mirth and his beak clacks, massive eyes squinting into an imitation of a human smile. Hoyt stifles a laugh, grinning between us. "It is a pleasure to meet my mate's friend." Kirby holds out a tentacle as if he wants to shake hands with Hoyt.

Hoyt shakes the tentacle, making a muffled "ooh" sound and giving me a wide-eyed appreciative glance and a none-too-discrete thumbs up when Kirby's suckers taste the flesh of his palm. And I shouldn't be jealous of that touch. There is nothing sexual about it. Except I know how amazing Kirby's suckers feel, how he seemed to taste me through them in the throes of passion, and I want them to be all mine. He is mine as much as I'm his.

"So, you're a kraken? Never met one before."

"Yes." Kirby burbles a trilling note, reminiscent of dolphins in a nature documentary. He makes all kinds of surprising noises. His crest puffs up with something I can't help interpreting as pride.

"And you're mated to Tris?" Hoyt presses.

"I am."

"Good. He's lucky to have found such a fearsome mate and protector. You are aware of the sirens living in the cove, right?" Hoyt asks.

"Of course." Kirby waves a tentacle dismissively. "Harmless creatures, if a touch vain. They will not lure my mate, or any of the other humans who are under our protection."

"Under your protection?" Hoyt looks startled.

"Yes, this is my territory. The human ships in it know to pay homage to me and in return, I ensure no harm comes to them or theirs from the sea."

His words trip me up, reminding me of a headline from last summer. A rescue operation after a toddler fell off a fishing vessel and was missing for days. They were still calling the search a rescue operation well beyond the point when everyone knew there was a vanishingly small hope of even recovering the boy's body. Except, three days after he fell overboard, they'd found him miraculously afloat on a spar of driftwood at the inlet to the harbor where his father's vessel docked.

The hospital treated him for hypothermia and dehydration, but he didn't have a scratch on him beyond that. Everyone called it a miracle, and the boy talked about an angel telling him to hold on to the wood and singing to him through the terrifying ordeal. It's not the only strange tale of remarkable survival in the area.

Ships finding their way to safe harbor during storms crediting a strange light for guiding them home. A scaled serpentine shadow propelling a stalled boat shoreward. A tourist caught in the undertow and swept out to sea, only to wash ashore with fantastical tales of merfolk singing to them beneath the waves. If you listened to the local gossip, that was just a few instances of the miraculous interventions that occurred along this stretch of ocean.

"You? You protect our town?" I ask.

Fuck, as if his skills at dicking me down weren't attractive enough. There is simply no way I can resist him if he's also some sort of superhero unseen protector.

"Not just me, but yes. The folks of Bellweather remember the old ways and we honor them in return. That's why I thought you must have understood the significance of vowing yourself to a sea marriage," Kirby explains. "Offering yourself to the sea isn't something anyone on shore would take lightly."

"I had no idea." I shake my head at how terribly wrong that little ritual could have gone if Kirby were any other sea monster. Not that I know much about what lives beneath the waves or any of the other cryptids I didn't believe were real until this week.

What if I'd promised myself to the sort of kraken you see in the movies, who delights in carnage and tearing apart ships and flesh with equal ease? I shiver, imagining Kirby holding me aloft by limbs strong enough to tear me asunder in a far less sexy way than he has split me apart thus far. The thought of his sheer strength shouldn't have my dick getting hard, but it does. He's just so powerful in so many senses.

"Yes, I gathered that when you didn't realize we were mated." Kirby sounds more amused than irritated with my ignorance by now, at least.

"I must have gotten my rituals crossed; I swear I thought it was just a stronger protection charm, or I would have warned you. The text I found isn't in the best shape." Hoyt rubs apologetically at the back of his neck and then gives me a hopeful smile. "All's well that ends well, though, right?"

"You're lucky I like him, Hoyt." I cross my arms and try to paste on a frown of consternation that can't quite reach my eyes. If not for Hoyt and his protection ritual, I'd never have known monsters are real. I would never have met Kirby, who seems increasingly like the perfect match the more I see of him.

"Oh, I'd say you more than like him, hmm?" Hoyt's eyes sparkle as he looks pointedly at the fresh line of sucker marks on my neck. I brush my fingers over the marks, fondly remembering our lovemaking earlier. Yeah, there's no denying I am more than alright with my sea monster lover.

"I'm not discussing our love life." I sniff and look away, playing at a prudishness I've never expressed with Hoyt about anyone else. But Kirby is different. And he's standing right there, as much as a boneless mollusk can be said to stand. Poised in my entryway with his massive tentacles balled up under him.

"Of course." Hoyt winks at me. "Not while your husband is right there watching, might make that big—ego—of his swell."

Kirby gives a delighted chirp, his tentacles twining over each other in a sensual slide. Fuck, I love the things those dextrous limbs can do to me. And my dick does too. A lot. In a fruitless effort to hide my arousal from Kirby and Hoyt, I turn on my heel to stride back into the kitchen. "Dinner is getting cold. Come, eat."

The two of them follow me to the table. Hoyt brought wine and caviar, so Kirby grabs the glasses and more bowls and spoons for the treat. Hoyt comments on how wonderful everything looks as we dish up bowls of soup, slices of warm bread, and exchange the usual pleasantries about the food and our days.

"Oh, that reminds me!" I break into Hoyt telling Kirby about his job as a cryptid adventure tour guide. "Brad and I heard your interview on Overnights with Orion."

Hoyt grins. "Ori is a character, isn't he? I always enjoy going on his show. Have to be careful with how much of the truth to share, obviously, but it's fun to have a wider audience. Plus, it always gets me a bump in business when we collaborate. He's hoping to get national syndication, you know?"

"Oh?"

"Yeah, I know the local station's exclusivity clause ran out in the spring. He's been working on a deal with a regional broadcaster ever since, so that would be wicked cool."

"Sure."

"What? You like the show, and now that you know that there's truth behind it and we're not all a bunch of credulous conspiracy-minded weirdos…"

"Hey! I never called you credulous."

"Uh huh, I see you don't dispute the rest of it?"

"I mean, if the shoe fits." I shrug and gesture at him. Hoyt presses both hands to his heart and pouts at me.

"I am wounded that you would go there. Those of us afflicted with small feet have no control over it, my dear sir."

"You are a silly man-child about your shoes. No one even notices."

Hoyt snorts, but the hurt in his face looks real. I might have overstepped by teasing him about that particular topic when I know it's a sore spot. It's just wild to me that a guy like him would worry about what his shoes say about his masculinity. He literally faces what I now know to be actual, real, potentially person-eating monsters for his job, for fuck's sake.

"You only say that because you don't have to shop in the little boy's section at shoe stores, Tris," Hoyt says ruefully. "And people *do* notice. Not every stranger on the street, but guys pick up on these things."

"Shallow guys who aren't good enough for you," I insist stubbornly. Even though I know part of his concern is about safety as much as it is wounded pride from being rejected by his dates over something so petty.

"Eh, agree to disagree." Hoyt bites a huge chunk off his slice of fresh bread. He moans around the mouthful in a way that has me questioning the sanity of any guy who would reject him, because he's a catch in so many ways.

Too bad we want different things in bed and a partner, or I'd have made a move ages ago. Then again, it's probably a stroke of luck, given that Kirby is perfect for me in every way that matters. Other than the parts where he is a writhing ball of tentacles who can't even pretend to pass for human. Still, sitting at my table with him and my best friend, I'm finding that matters to me less and less.

Hoyt gestures with the rest of his bread. "This is delicious. You are wasted in your hospital dungeon lair."

"Eh, I like my lair. If you like it so much, I made a big bulk batch before the move. There should be plenty still in the freezer for you to take home. Baking would be stressful if I tried to do it for a living. I prefer going to bed at dawn to waking up that early, for one thing. Bakers' hours are for the birds."

"Well, you already caught yourself several nice juicy worms, you lucky boy." Hoyt winks at me, eyeing up Kirby's tentacles salaciously as my mate slurps delicately from his bowl.

"You mean my tentacles?" Kirby asks, all innocence. "He has sampled them quite enthusiastically, yes. My mate has a very healthy appetite."

I pretend to hide my face in my hands, peeking between two fingers, as Hoyt smirks and Kirby all but preens at getting to crow about his prowess. "Humans don't discuss our sex lives over dinner, Kirby."

"No? But your friend brought it up. And in your books they do," Kirby says.

"I *did* bring it up first." Hoyt nods as he throws me under the bus.

"Those books aren't realistic," I protest, squirming in my seat. Which of course has the plug nudging my prostate. That shouldn't feel so good so soon after Kirby fucked me damn near senseless, but it does.

"Ah. So, we will not provide a demonstration of your—attributes?" Kirby asks, deadpan.

"No! Nope." I wave my hands, inarticulate with mortification even as Hoyt tries to disguise his amusement at my mate's lack of human social skills. I take a long moment to realize that they're teasing me, the pair of jerks. And fuck, now I'm hyperaware of still being full of Kirby's cum and the plug. "No demonstrations of any kind!"

"Ah, so you don't want me to show you the—"

"Nope!" I glare.

Hoyt looks like he might burst from trying to hide his amusement. His smile is all twinkly and aglow with delight as he glances between Kirby and me. It's like he knows that two of Kirby's tentacles have found my ankles under the table, rubbing up and down my shins.

"Sooooo," I draw out the word, desperate to shift the conversation back to Hoyt and his reasons for asking to meet with us tonight. This thing with Kirby, all the new horizons sex with a sea monster has opened for me, is still too new and tender to share. I'm facing so many new facets of myself; I'm not ready for them to be the subject of friendly banter. Not yet.

"You mentioned the recent increase in animal attacks on your radio segment. Do you know what's causing them?" I ask, hoping a more serious topic will help rein in my ardor for Kirby. "That's one area where you had to be careful not to reveal too much, right?"

Hoyt sighs and sets aside his spoon, sobering instantly. "Yeah. Or rather, I know what isn't causing the incidents. The local cryptids aren't behind the attacks. At least, no one who is on the council's radar. They have a way of knowing their own. Self-governance, you know?" Hoyt gestures at Kirby. "Like how the local fishers give sacrifices to the sea to appease your mate there and he keeps his people in line in exchange."

The kraken bobs sagely, tentacles waving eagerly. "Yes, the sea folks know our territory and who may and may not pass through it. We also know where we may hunt and which humans are off limits."

I shudder at the thought that any human might be my mate's natural prey. I don't want to think of him eating people.

Kirby squinches his strange, swirling eyes at me and clacks his beak. "I do not partake in sentient flesh." He slurps pointedly at his soup. "But there are some creatures who prefer the old ways."

"Sirens?" Hoyt probes eagerly.

Kirby's crest wobbles, and he whistles out a breath. "Not our local chorus. There is a kelpie who likes to toy with the tourists, but he knows not to hunt on our shores. And a particularly malicious sea sprite who we had to drive from the shallows when the people made offerings to protect their young from the deep."

"I see, and Cassie?"

"The serpent does not venture into my territory. One of her young some-times visits." Kirby sounds almost fond when he says that. Like he cares about the baby sea serpent. It shouldn't be, but sometimes it's easy to forget just how inhuman my mate truly is.

"Agh, you are a treasure trove about the creatures of the deep, Kirby, darling. I think you and I will be fast friends." Hoyt tips his glass toward Kirby, who bobs in an eager imitation of a human nod.

"Yes. You are my mate's companion. We will both care for Tristan."

"We will." Hoyt nods, then he reaches over to ruffle my hair. Rude. But I lean into the affection.

Kirby coils his tentacle more firmly around my ankle. The tip slips under my pants to wrap around bare flesh, as if he needs to touch me more. Taste my skin. That makes my heart all warm and fluttery. It might not be conventional, but I have a mate who makes me feel cherished and loved. The fact his tentacles are a part of that love isn't anyone's business.

"Which is why I needed to meet with you both. I know the underwater cryptids rarely make it onto hunter's radar for any number of reasons. But there's been a recent increase in potential cryptid sighting reports. Attacks being blamed on local creatures in certain corners of the internet fits an ominous pattern. We—that is those affiliated with the cryptid community among humanity—have noticed them using similar strategies elsewhere."

"You are a Watcher?" Kirby asks.

"Yes." Hoyt nods. I am lost, and he seems to realize it, placing a hand over mine. "There's a bit more to my job than escorting tourists into the woods and giving them a good time."

"I knew that. But, how do you, like, keep the actual cryptids safe, if you're revealing their secrets to the masses?"

Hoyt rolls his eyes. "It's not like we actually capture solid evidence. The cryptids who work with me are all stealth, for one thing. We carefully curate what the tourists experience, tailored to each tour group. We generally have clients who fall into three broad categories."

"Yeah? You mean everyone doesn't come to you looking for their very own sexy monster to fuck?"

"No, I'd have made an exception for you though, Tris." Hoyt winks at me. I pout at him, which only makes him chuckle and shake his head before he ticks his categories off on his fingers.

"First, we have the true believers. Those come in two flavors. The ones who will never quite get enough from their experience, no matter how much we reveal, and those who are happy to see whatever we want them to see. That includes the monster fuckers like you." Hoyt winks at me again.

"Then there are skeptics of varying degrees who want an experience to tell their friends about. They're like the first group, looking for a narrative more than solid proof either way. And last there are the hunters." Hoyt's brow furrows. "They're looking for real, hard evidence. Not that cryptids are real—they already know—but who and where they are. They try to find or create cracks in our cryptids' connection to the community so they can exploit them."

"Exploit them how?" I don't like the sound of that at all. Are there hunters out there looking for Kirby right now? What would they even do with him?

I squeeze my ankles together around Kirby, where he's grasping onto me. The protective urge toward the big monster surprises me, but I lean into it, he's my mate as much as I'm his. Even if I'm still not entirely sure what that means for our future, I want Kirby to be safe.

"Kraken slime has regenerative properties. It can be refined into a potent healing brew," Hoyt says. As if that's not a fresh layer of mind-blowing on top of the past few days' revelations about the nature of reality.

"Is he in danger?" I reach protectively for my mate. The motion jostles the plug in my ass, reminding me again of what we share. New and precarious as that bond is, I don't want to lose it. I certainly don't want anything bad to happen to Kirby because of his interest in me.

Kirby coils a tentacle around my wrist, warbling a pleased sound at my concern. Or maybe trying to soothe me? I'm still learning to read him. Of course, I'm worried about his safety. Even if he wasn't my mate, he's clearly highly intelligent, and no one deserves to have illicit experiments done on them in some actual basement lair.

Hoyt snorts, and Kirby clacks his beak defiantly

"I am perfectly safe, mate." Kirby's tentacle crawls up my arm and along my neck, stroking soothingly over the sucker marks he left all over me. His slime can't be all that powerful at healing, considering how clearly I can see the evidence of our lovemaking.

"He's right." Hoyt nods. "Krakens are usually more dangerous than they're worth the attempt to capture. Not to mention the difficulty of containing them once they are taken. They need access to ocean water and natural tides to thrive, and are better escape artists than their octopus cousins. The Houdinis of the sea, if you will. And anyway, voluntarily imbuing their slime with healing properties is much harder to make use of compared to what they do to other cryptids with more easy to harvest resources."

"Like what?" I ask, horrified at the thought of harming a creature like Kirby. That explains his marks lingering on my body. If the healing properties are under his volitional control, Kirby left his marks on me because he wanted to.

I rub a thumb over my wrist, thrilling at the reawakened tenderness. Or perhaps he left the marks because he'd observed how much those parts of my favorite stories turn me on. It also explains how I took several of his thick limbs inside my ass with only a pleasant ache to remind me of it as I sit at the table.

"Well, for one, were-packs can communicate uncannily over long distances using pheromones. Not to mention their healing factor puts a kraken's to shame, since they need ridiculous levels of regenerative proliferation to survive a full shift, let alone doing it at will. And the hunters have a particular fondness for their enhanced strength and senses. We're just lucky that the myths of being able to transmit shifter genes through a bite are not based in reality. If the hunters could become shifters or create their own super shifter soldiers, it would make protecting our communities more challenging, that's for certain."

"Doesn't that just make shifters more of a target, though? So they can hire or otherwise entice their cooperation?"

Hoyt nods, a sad frown on his face. "It happens. Most cryptid communities are good about safeguarding their youth against the sort of grooming that can happen with hunters to recruit young cryptids eager for acceptance in human society. But it helps that most hunters consider cryptids so far beneath them that they would rather avoid working with them. Or even using them in the same capacity as one might train a hunting dog. In fact, they are more likely to hunt with perfectly mundane animals than cryptids, willing recruits or otherwise."

"I guess that's a silver lining?"

"It is." Hoyt nods. "But the thing is, our local cryptid community appears to have caught the attention of some hunters. I've tracked an uptick in the amount of chatter in their usual online haunts and several mentions of Bellweather and our local cryptids. So we have been doing our best to muddle their efforts at drumming up the sort of rumors that can turn a community against itself."

"Huh? But I thought most people don't even know about or believe in monsters."

Hoyt nods. "Sure, but they have a pattern for taking peaceful cryptids from their homes. Whether it's a corporate interest or a more covert group, they use similar tactics. First there are far-fetched rumors. And then they spread stories about the local cryptids being a threat to public safety, but with an underlying mundane explanation. Animal attacks or drownings, whatever fits the behavior patterns of the target creatures. And then, once they've spread enough fear, they rile up the community about the cover story. Then they swoop in and offer to make the problem go away before the folks in the mainstream discover the truth about their cryptid neighbors."

"You think all those animal attacks we've been treating are part of an effort to creature-nap local monsters?"

"I wouldn't quite word it like that—they're people, not creatures—but essentially, yes. Which is why I needed to go on Ori's show. To get the word out to the community that it's a real good time to hunker down and not make any waves, so to speak. With the high profile of Craig Delmare's mysterious presumed drowning and now the uptick in admissions to the hospital for bite wounds, it's not looking good. That's part of why my sister and her family postponed their visit."

"But would they really be at risk?"

"It depends on what the hunters are here to accomplish. But the kids don't always have the best control of their abilities. People might notice and think it's harmless to share how they saw a cute child seeming to make flowers blossom in her hair. But if the wrong person learns about their heritage..."

"They're little kids!" I protest.

Hoyt's mouth sets in a grim line. "That makes them easier to control. They haven't bonded to a tree yet, so it makes them much easier to uproot than an adult dryad. That's why these folks are so insidious. And the thing is, they can make the benefit to society sound worth the cost. What is one child cooperating with them while their family is well-compensated for their seemingly harmless contributions against a potential cure for cancer?"

"Is that even what they're working on?"

"Not generally, no. But they have derived some very inventive—not to mention profitable—herbicides from captive nymphs. Medications aren't outside the realm of possibility. It's happened before."

I nod, mentally cataloging various plant-derived medications from taxanes for cancer, to aspirin from willow bark to digitalis, theophylline, and more. Or even migraine treatments from ergot alkaloids made by a fungus that infects grain. What would it mean if you had a researcher who could purify medicinal isolates by simply requesting it from the plants in question? It defies reason. And as miraculous as the idea sounds, it's still not worth the cost of exploiting little children to achieve that end.

Besides, I'd like to think if it were really as simple as asking their plants, the dryads would have done as much already. Perhaps some innovations have resulted from truly willing collaborations. I'd like to hope so.

"Are there hunters here?" Kirby asks, several of his tentacles lashing irritably along my floor, reminding me of an angry cat's tail.

"Not yet. Or at least, not that we've detected. I'm not the only Watcher in the area. We've been working closely with the local council of land cryptids. But part of why I asked Tris to introduce us is that there are some rumors circulating about Craig and the boy your people rescued last year. The one who fell from his father's fishing boat. Strange miracles on the open water. So there is every chance they are targeting a creature that falls under your purview."

"Or someone with amphibious leanings, if they are muddying the waters, so to speak, between creatures that live on the land and in the ocean."

"Hm, maybe a selkie? They are usually pacifists, unlikely to harm anyone, so a bite attack seems like a strange way to vilify them," Kirby muses. "Perhaps a kelpie? I will put out the word among the sea folks."

"They both seem more likely to be behind drowning deaths than the attacks we've been seeing. It's impossible to say who these hunters are targeting without more information. I just wanted to make sure you are aware of the dangers." Hoyt gives us a tight smile.

Kirby bobs his crest in a nod. "I will warn the sea folk to remain vigilant. Thank you for the warning. We will report any strange activity within our territory. We shall meet again soon to share any new information that comes to light."

"Oh, for sure. I'll be back to visit plenty." Hoyt winks, then slings an arm around my shoulders so he can hold me still to muss my hair affectionately—the infuriating man. "Tris has been my best friend since we were kids. We even roomed together at university. Overachiever here went for several years longer than the rest of us. Did he tell you he's a doctor?"

Hoyt reaches to cut another slice of bread, then leans back in his seat to watch how that tidbit lands.

"Is he?" Kirby makes a delighted chirruping sound. "My mate is pretty and smart."

I roll my eyes. "Only on paper. It's still an entry level degree and pretty much no one uses the title. It's fine, makes us more accessible to the public."

"You still earned it," Hoyt points out, brandishing his fresh slice of bread at me. This is an old argument that I will not win. I act exasperated, but it gives me the warm fuzzies to be acknowledged. Especially in front of my mate.

Even when he pushes all my buttons, Hoyt is the best friend everyone should be so lucky as to have. He makes me feel cared about and seen, and is there to celebrate my wins with me. Even if my current win is accidentally getting mated off to a sea monster. The very best, sexiest sea monster in the ocean, but still.

He's got tentacles and magical healing sex slime, and Hoyt doesn't seem to care in the least as long as Kirby makes me happy.

And so far, he does. Even when he's making me sit as still as possible across from my best friend because I'm trying not to make it obvious I've got a plug up my ass. Mm. I bite my lip, it's so damn hot to know I'm holding in my mate's load. Hoyt would find that revelation hilarious, so the stakes have more to do with the embarrassment of sharing than truly needing to keep our game private.

Our game. Because I have a mate who shares my fantasies. Now I just need to wrap my head around the fact that I want to stay mated to my kraken. Even if there was a simple way out, I'm so far past the point of wanting it. The shared meal with my best friend and my mate clinches it. This is a snapshot of the life and future I want to build for myself.

I can live without the whole town knowing my business as long as I can share Kirby with the people who matter to me. Hoyt, his family, and a select few of our other friends and loved ones. Someday maybe I can even share him with my sister and nephew, who live out of state. But for now, watching my best friend and my lover bonding is enough.

"Since Tris can't bring you around town, we'll just have to get acquainted here. Like you said, you and I are going to be friends, Kirby." Hoyt echoes my thoughts.

It's good to see them getting along. I'm caught between wanting to soak up every second of this evening and the intense longing to be alone with my kraken. As soon as Hoyt leaves, Kirby will unplug me and fuck his cum right back out of my ass. It's going to be a very good night.

CHAPTER 13

Cake by the ocean/Sex on the Beach

After dinner, Hoyt hangs out with Kirby and me on the beach for a while. Hoyt starts out treating Kirby as if he were just like any of my past boyfriends. Friendly surface level teasing. Except, the two of them get along so much better than Hoyt and most of my exes. That goes a long way to making this seem all the more real. Like Kirby is someone I can build a future with on the basis of more than the epic sex.

Sure, we might not be able to have date nights at the local bar, but I've always been such a homebody that I doubt I'll miss those outings. And I can still hang out in town with friends if I ever do.

We end up on the beach, sitting near the surf in heavy wooden Adirondack chairs that came with the property. Kirby trails his tentacles into the waves. He moves with even more powerful elegance in the water than out of it, continually drawing my eyes to his every movement. He's a picture of predatory grace.

I crack open the sparkling wine and pour us each a glass. We toast to Hoyt's interview with Orion and his efforts to keep the cryptid community safe and Kirby and my mating. We finish a second bottle—well, mostly me. Kirby seems to enjoy the novelty of the bubbles more than the actual beverage, and Hoyt has to drive.

"Can I pour you another round?" I hold up the bottle to Hoyt as I top off my glass.

"Better not, I need to get home sometime tonight."

"Pshaw, you are always welcome to crash on the couch." I wiggle the bottle enticingly, as if the plug I'm wearing isn't getting uncomfortable.

Hoyt guffaws, glancing meaningfully between Kirby and where I'm squirming in my seat to get comfortable with the plug again. "Not tonight. Maybe when you two are past the horny newlywed stage, we can revisit that invite." He winks at me, and I can't deny that I am more than ready to jump my invertebrate lover's bones as soon as we're alone again. "I brought something else for you, in case you seemed ready to celebrate this mating? Happy looks good on you, Tris."

Hoyt stands and leans in to pat my cheek affectionately.

"Oh? I won't say no to presents." I make grabby hands at him. Hoyt chuckles.

"I'll grab it. Left it in the car in case Kirby turned out to be a wrecker of hearts as well as ships." Hoyt gives us both a cheeky wink and jogs toward his car.

He returns carrying a plain box from the cute little bakery on Main Street, next to Aroma Joe's. Kirby puffs up, tentacles questing toward whatever is inside.

"What did you bring?" Kirby asks, crest puffed curiously.

"You didn't have to bring anything else, Hoyt."

"I wanted to. It's nothing fancy, but according to human traditions, marriage includes celebrating your union with cake." He opens the box and presents it to us with a flourish. Inside is a small cake frosted in a neon blue and aquamarine ombre with bright pink corals piped onto the top.

I can't help laughing at the little plastic figures he clearly stuck into the colorful frosting himself. A LEGO person in a lab coat stands next to a chunky Cthulhu figure I recognize from his bookshelf.

"I didn't have an actual kraken, so I had to improvise." Hoyt shrugs self-consciously as he folds the box flaps out of the way to give us both an unobstructed view of the most perfect little ocean-themed wedding cake. "What do you think?"

"It's perfect, Hoyt." I'm surprised at how choked up I'm getting over his kind gesture.

"Smells delicious. I approve of this human mating tradition." Kirby makes a pleased humming noise.

It's not like I spent my teen years dreaming about a fantasy wedding. I generally don't care about following social norms that make no sense and seem like more of a hassle than they're worth. But Hoyt giving his blessing to my relationship with Kirby, as untraditional and fast-moving as it is, means the world to me.

"Yeah? Glad you like it. Should I take a picture of the two happy grooms eating their wedding cake by the shore?" Hoyt offers, holding up his phone. "Just for the two of you."

Kirby and I share a glance.

"You know you want him to stuff your face, Tris." Hoyt winks. And I can't help jumping to much pervier thoughts of exactly how I want Kirby to stuff all of my holes. Later. After Hoyt leaves. The giant brat knows exactly what he's doing, making comments like that. The plug is really getting to me. A growing part of me wants Hoyt to leave so Kirby can finally remove it and make good on his earlier promises.

Kirby chortles, the sound reminding me of a cross between a bird and whale song. He swipes a tentacle through the frosting and presses it to my lips. "I am always happy to feed you, my mate."

I barely notice the flash of Hoyt's phone snapping photos of us as Kirby guides a morsel of cake between my lips. The mix of his salty ocean tang mixed with sweet buttercream makes me shiver with need for him. I delight in the luscious creaminess of frosting over his muscular digit pushing into my mouth for me to suck him clean. Damn, the sheer sensuality of the moment has my cock plumping and I fidget in my chair, jostling the infernal plug. As if I needed any reminder of just how gone I am for the kraken before me.

Hoyt snaps more pictures as I scoop up a handful of the cake to feed Kirby. I smear it over his beak as his long tongue presses firm against my palm. His touch lights up every nerve between my hand and my dick.

"Right." Hoyt clears his throat. "Great pictures. Think I should take my slice to go so you two can get back to the honeymoon?"

"Stay, enjoy the cake with us," Kirby says, sweeping an inviting tentacle toward Hoyt's chair even as his huge swirling eyes twinkle with mischief.

"Yes, stay a little longer." I casually pluck the Cthulhu figure off the top of the cake and lick the frosting off of it, just a little salaciously. Might as well tease Hoyt back for all his playful prodding.

"Just for cake, then I should get going, anyway. I have a tour tomorrow to prepare for." Hoyt dishes up three thick slices, then folds the box back together around the rest of the cake, the better to ward off the seagulls circling overhead. I'm sure Kirby's hulking presence is all that's held them back from stealing their own bites of cake thus far. Grabby birds.

I sip my bubbly wine and nibble at the delicious cake, enjoying the perfect night. The breeze off the ocean is cold, but I'm cozy, wrapped in a warm blanket and sharing an evening with two of my favorite people.

It's nice to take some time to be together, time with Kirby that isn't spent tangled in his tentacles. Over our cake, Kirby and Hoyt take turns telling me increasingly improbable stories about the various wonders of the world that I never believed existed before. Hoyt seems eager when Kirby suggests introducing us to more of the sea folk, and so am I. Even beyond my natural curiosity about Kirby's world, I want to meet his friends.

The conversation moves on, with the two of them acting like little boys competing to tell the most shocking story. Poor Hoyt doesn't stand a chance of outdoing Kirby in my eyes, despite his years as a cryptozoologist. For one thing, Kirby gesticulating with all of his tentacles as he talks is mesmerizing. Hoyt notices the thirsty way I'm staring and pokes fun at me.

"God, you are such a slut for his tentacles. Can't you keep it in your pants until I go home?" He nudges me in the ribs playfully.

"Yes." I pout, then bat my eyes at him. "Apropos of nothing, weren't you heading out soon?"

Hoyt laughs, shaking his head ruefully as he sets his frosting smeared plate on top of the cake box. "I see how it is; I'll let you two get back to, uh, celebrating. Do this again soon?"

Hoyt reaches to pocket the little cake topper figures.

"Absolutely." I stand to say a proper goodbye. "See you soon."

"I'd wish you a good night, but I'm sure you've got that more than covered." Hoyt hugs me, then sort of offers a handshake to Kirby, only to be wrapped in tentacles for a back-slapping kraken version of a bro hug. Hoyt's smiling and whistling cheerily to himself as he heads back to his car.

Kirby uses his tentacles to pull himself up my body, so that he can nuzzle his beak next to my ear as we both watch Hoyt go.

"You're being so good waiting for me, my mate." Kirby pats my head with one long limb and I shiver in anticipation of just where I want that trailing touch to lead. But Kirby just rests there, his bulk draped over my shoulder as we watch Hoyt adjusting his mirrors. I'm pretty sure he is drawing out his departure as a form of best friend torture.

I listen to the crunch of Hoyt's tires reversing over my gravel drive and then his headlights sweep over the little patch of beach where we're sitting, heralding his departure. Kirby's affectionate touches shift to something more sensual—and more forceful. I welcome the way his tentacles wrap around me, his suckers fastening onto my wrists, marking me anew with a cuff of his love bites. I want them inked indelibly into my skin. A permanent reminder of our mating. That actually sounds like a good idea; a tattoo might make his marks less noticeable to outside observers.

I mean, if I really am sure about this. It's probably too soon to consider making permanent body modifications for him, but I care about Kirby. I want to have a future with him in it. Not just because of the incredible sex either. He was just as witty and charming with Hoyt as he's been when it's just the two of us. He helped me with the housework without having to be asked. Heck, he's been protecting the people of Bellweather out of some ancient code of honor most folks have probably long forgotten exists.

I am undeniably falling hard for my kraken. And he's got me wrapped so tight in his coils that I'm in danger of literally falling too. How freeing to realize I trust him implicitly to catch me in both senses. His thick, powerful limbs manhandle me toward the chair, bending me over the back and sliding up my legs under my pants. Kirby's limbs slipping into my clothing alongside my legs stretch the fabric tight and add an unfamiliar dimension to the sense of constriction around each limb as his tentacles thicken to take up more space alongside mine.

Kirby spreads my thighs wide and one tentacle loops around my balls, suckers fastening on tight even as two more delicate appendages nudge the plug lodged in my ass. He rocks it into my prostate before probing my rim alongside the thick rubber. Threatening to stretch me wide and plumb my depths yet again.

I'm not sure if I have it in me to take him again so soon. My balls ache from coming so much in the past few days, my hole is tender from a thorough fuck earlier and the plug still stretching me. If what Hoyt said about kraken slime's healing properties is true, then I can only imagine how sore I'd be without that magical boost. But I feel well used and pleasantly achy as Kirby coaxes my cock to full mast and teases my hole.

Kirby has my arms pinned to my sides. His suckers move rhythmically over my flesh. He finds all my sensitive spots and pays them extra attention, the most thorough lover imaginable. I vacillate between thinking his single-minded focus on me is too intense, and that I'll never be able to get my fill of him.

Kirby pushes my pants down to expose the base of the plug nestled inside me. He breaches me with a thin tendril of one of his tentacle tips so that he can push the plug out, freeing a warm gush of his release from earlier.

"Hold still while I prepare you, mate."

Before I can adequately respond, he lowers his face to my pucker and laps at the fluids slicking my hole. The implicit threat of his serrated beak so close to tender flesh has me shivering with anticipation. His muscular tongue presses against my rim. In no time, his insistent licking has me seeing stars.

Mindful of his command, I struggle not to squirm as he lathes my rim, probing gently at the delicate flesh, keeping the edges of his beak at a careful distance. Then his long tongue delves deeper as he starts tongue-fucking me. Kirby eats my ass on the beach like I'm even more of a delicacy than the cake we just shared. He rims me until I'm a mess of sobbing need, begging him to fill me up and fuck his come back out of me for real. He works one, then two, then three of his tentacles in alongside his tongue.

"Oh! More!" I moan, and Kirby keeps fucking me like the needy slut I am.

"Oh, yes. Relax and I'll give you everything you can take, my mate."

I lean into his tight hold and just enjoy the way Kirby can crack me open and make me feel things I've never felt before. Cherished. Adored. And so thoroughly debauched I might never walk straight again if not for that healing kraken slime that seems to fill me to bursting. Kirby's cum drips down my thighs with every powerful pump of his tentacles slipping past each other inside of me.

Kirby is true to his earlier promise, fucking his come back out of me. He fucks me right to the brink of bliss and over the edge until I come with him buried inside me yet again. I orgasm so hard that I see stars other than the ones shining down on us from the clear night sky.

With the moon, stars, and the tides as our witnesses, my mate carries me gently back to my bed and tucks me in next to him. I can no longer deny, even to myself, that this is exactly what I want. A lifetime of spending my nights laughing with Kirby. Cooking with him, and entertaining our friends together.

More nights sharing cake by the ocean. And getting fucked senseless with his tentacles. A lifetime as his mate doesn't sound nearly as scary as it did at first. It's time to stop standing in the way of my own happiness, and I'm looking forward to knowing everything about the kraken in my bed.

EPILOGUE

Musseling in

I love my sister and her son. Except waking up to the sound of my nephew's pitter-pattering little feet pelting down my hall is a bit of a nightmare scenario right now. Lyle's enthusiastic knocking is a rude awakening just as Kirby is slowly coaxing me from drowsy lust-filled dreaming toward full consciousness. His tentacles are already exploring my body—two of them circling my cock while a third teases my hole. The honeymoon is far from over after nearly a month of having him in my bed.

Lyle calls out, "Uncle Tris!"

I groan at the interruption. I wasn't expecting Caroline to bring her son for a visit today. But I recall her mentioning Lyle has a long weekend off from school. When her husband got called away for a last-minute business trip, Caroline sounded disappointed to cancel their beach weekend. And she would know where to find the spare key in my new house. It's stuck on a nail tucked into an obscured corner of the siding, just like where our folks used to keep theirs.

So she must have decided it would be fun to surprise me. If not for Kirby, I'd have invited her to bring the kid around, no problem.

I bite my lip as my mate's tentacles withdraw. I really wanted to get fucked, but I swallow the curse on the tip of my tongue. My heart is racing, because how do I explain a kraken in my bedroom to my sister? Let alone a kid who might not understand the dire risks if he can't keep his mouth shut about cryptids?

Then again, I want to tell them both about my mate. I want to share how happy he's been making me. How right this mating feels. I want Kirby to be a part of my family and that means eventually introducing him to the other parts of my family. Not just Hoyt.

I can hear my sister talking to her son right outside my door now, so I scramble out of bed and pull on my bathrobe. I've been going to bed naked to better enjoy the way Kirby's tentacles wrap around me when we sleep. Caro and Lyle don't need to see my sucker marks, no matter how much I love them.

"Tris? You up?" Caroline raps her knuckles on my door, ever the bossy big sister.

"Uh, yeah. Sorry. You startled me." I dart my eyes around the room and fix on the window. Kirby can probably sneak back out to the ocean that way. He's done it before. I make eye contact with my mate and furiously gesture. He ignores me.

"Is that your sister?" Kirby asks, not as quietly as I'd prefer.

"Yes. You should, uh…" I trail off, because I really don't want to be the sort of person who tells my husband he has to hide from my family. But what if it isn't safe for him? I tug at my hair.

Caro is one of the kindest people I know. She loves all things seafood, but refuses to eat octopus because of their intelligence. And krakens are several steps beyond their animal cousins. She won't do anything to hurt Kirby. I have to believe that.

Kirby wilts as my unfinished sentence hangs in the air between us. He slumps dejectedly out of our bed and I grab for one of his trailing tentacles. "I can leave if that is your wish." He tugs half-heartedly against my grip and I squeeze him.

"No. I want them to meet you. If you aren't worried about them saying something to the wrong people." I drop my voice even further. "With the hunters around, we can't be too careful." Just thinking about their ominous presence in our town makes my hair stand on end. I want Kirby—and the other cryptids in our community—to be safe.

"Tris? Is someone in there with you?" Caroline sounds...well, she sounds excited, while also being scandalized that I didn't tell her I'm seeing someone.

"Um. Yeah."

"Well, get dressed and come introduce him. I'll make coffee."

"Bless you," I call through the door. Coffee makes everything better. Usually. Hopefully, even telling my sister that monsters are real and I'm married to one.

"But I wanted to show Uncle Tris my new Octolord!" Lyle whines.

"Come on, Lyle. Uncle Tris has a new boyfriend; let's give them a minute of privacy since we barged in on them, yeah? You can show him your toy in the kitchen."

"Fine. Release the kraken!" Lyle's footsteps charge back down the hall at an exuberant pace as he makes what I can only assume are supposed to be Octolord sound effects. There are a lot of whooshing noises, roars, pew pews, and 'fire the lasers' being shouted.

"Agh, my leg!" Lyle exclaims.

"Is he alright?" Kirby asks me, eyes going wide and crest scrunching in with concern.

"Hi, brother's boyfriend!" Caroline is still standing right outside our bedroom. "Lyle is fine, quoting one of his shows." She chuckles. "The kid got your imagination, Tris, I swear. He's always making up stories about creepy crawlies. Don't let us scare you away. I'm the bossy sister I'm sure he's told you all about, and the kid is his nephew, in case that wasn't clear."

"It was," Kirby says. "My mate has told me all about his favorite sister and nephew."

Caroline snorts. "We're his only sister and nephew. It's weird chatting through the door. Get decent and come to the kitchen, baby brother."

"Yeah." I have no choice other than to go out there. Might as well try to put things off a little longer. "Coffee first?"

"Coffee first," Caroline agrees decisively.

Her footsteps retreat. Kirby gathers my clothing, holding a different garment in each limb and offering them all to me. I pull on my clothing mechanically, mind blank at the prospect of how Caroline is going to react to Kirby. There's no avoiding it now. We've already committed. And I'm strangely okay with this.

Kirby straightens out my shirt, then he pulls me in for a hard and unyielding kiss. We've figured out our own take on the human gesture. His tentacles slither over my lips to shield them from the sharp edges of his beak as he presses it against my mouth so that our tongues can tangle. I still can't get enough of his musky sea salt tang.

"This will be okay, mate," he says, pulling away from me. And then he opens the door and goes to meet my family. I follow him down the hall.

The scent of the coffee percolating fills the air. My nephew sees Kirby first. His jaw drops and his cuddly kraken plush toy falls from his slack fingers.

"Oh-my-gosh! Mom! MOMMY! Uncle Kirby has a real kraken!" Lyle points, and then he runs up to Kirby before cautiously reaching out to prod one of his tentacles.

Kirby, without missing a beat, takes the boy's hand. He wraps a coil of his tentacles around Lyle's palm and gives him a jarringly human handshake just as Caro turns from fixing her cup of coffee to her satisfaction. She screams when she sees my mate too, though hers is more that of a terrified parent watching a sea monster with her child than Lyle's delighted glee.

Caroline's mug crashes to the ground in a spray of hot coffee and shattered ceramic. The mug is the least of my concerns, I can replace it. We'll have to clean up the sharp shards before they cut delicate tentacles or Lyle's feet. And that is more pressing, but it's really just a distraction from the sheer horror on my sister's face.

"Tris! There's a—a…" Caroline shakes her head, all but hyperventilating as she presses her hand over her mouth.

"Um, so Caro, this is Kirby. My mate—not my boyfriend. He's a kraken. Surprise?" I rub anxiously at his sucker marks on my wrists, hoping Caro won't freak out, snatch up her son, and leave without giving me a chance to explain.

The need to stim a whole lot more forcefully than the situation allows grips me, but I have to hold it together for now. It might mean I have a meltdown later tonight, but I can probably put that off until after we get our unexpected guests settled into the spare room. Once Caroline and Lyle go to bed, I can hole up in the quiet darkness of my bedroom. And if I can't make it that long, it won't be the end of the world.

Everyone here has seen me when I can't cope anymore. They'll still be my family on the other side, no matter how much I'd rather breakdown in private versus in front of them. I just really don't want to handle Caroline hating my husband. I sway a bit, still rubbing furiously at my sucker marked wrist until Kirby coils a tentacle tip soothingly around it, grounding me with the barest touch.

"Surprise?!" Caroline repeats, voice rising with an edge of hysteria. My sister looks like she might pass out from the shock, her face pale and breathing coming in sharp gasps. I hurriedly guide her toward a chair. Kirby gently lets go of my wrist when I move.

"Look, I have a kraken too! His name is Octolord, Terror of the Seventies." Lyle shows off his toy by shoving it into Kirby's face, seemingly oblivious to his mother's fear for his safety.

"Don't you mean seven seas?" Kirby asks, watching my nephew quizzically as the kid holds up his octopus plush toy.

"Nope!" Lyle shakes his head, gap-toothed grin on full display. "Dad said it's the seventies, because Octolord is psychedelic neon."

The toy is an eye-popping kaleidoscope swirl of colorful fabric

Caroline sinks into the seat I offer her, but then seems to get her second wind. "Surprise? Tristan, what the—" she cuts her gaze to where Kirby is keeping my nephew occupied, dancing the kraken toy across his tentacles as Lyle describes all the toy's fictional exploits. Kirby playing contentedly with her kid seems to calm her down. Caroline leans closer, all but hissing at me. "He talks! How is this possible?"

"So." I rub at the back of my neck. My fingers find a tender spot where Kirby left more of his sucker marks and the touch grounds me. "You know how Hoyt does cryptid tours and is always talking about monsters being real?"

"Yeah?" Caroline nods.

"Well, he convinced me to do a sort of protection ritual. Only we got the purpose wrong a little and it turned out to be a mating ritual."

"Mating? Tris! *He's* your boyfriend? He's..." The penny drops, and she buries her face into her hands. Caro groans. I don't correct the terminology again, boyfriend is close enough while she gets used to my relationship with Kirby. "He's like a character out of your trashy sci-fi romances."

"He's a person," I protest. On some level, I crave my big sister's approval, so in a more wheedling tone, I add, "Sure, he's also a kraken, but he makes me happy, Caro."

"Yeah?" She peeks at me between her fingers, her face flushed.

"Yeah. He's kind and funny and his tentacles—"

"Whoa!" Caroline holds up a hand to halt me. "I do not want to know the details of where any of those tentacles have been. But if he makes you happy—and isn't planning to devour my son—then I'm happy for you, Tristan."

"The only devouring he wants to do to humans falls under things you don't want to hear about my love life, sis." I wink at her, because I'm far more interested in Kirby's tentacles than any sort of blow job.

"Gag."

"So, I wasn't expecting to see you two today." I change the subject.

"Oh, yeah. Carl was supposed to take us to the cape for the long weekend. But he had his emergency work trip, so I figured kiddo and I could still make the most of the school break by seeing you and enjoying the unseasonable warmth for one last beach weekend."

That explanation checks out. Caro's husband travels for work a lot. My sister and her son both love the water, so they hardly need any excuse to finagle a few days on the shore. Sure, I'd have appreciated some warning, but Kirby and I were planning to entertain anyway. Since the holiday lines up with Sukkot, Hoyt's sister and niblings are in town too, so of course I'm having everyone over for a beach cookout.

I grab my Swiffer to mop up the spilled coffee and throw out the broken mug. Caroline gets over her initial shock and interrogates me about Kirby and the existence of monsters. Kirby keeps my nephew occupied playing some sort of pirate game.

Caroline helps me finish cleaning and I fix us fresh mugs of coffee before getting out food for the cookout Kirby and I had already planned. We got plenty of food, so a couple of extra guests shouldn't be a problem. I lay everything for our meal out on the counter. We have chips, Maine's signature red hot dogs with New England style buns, and burger patties that Kirby helped me prep before we went to bed. Everything is ready to go and Hoyt should be arriving soon.

As we complete the final food prep, I share the gossip about my new relationship with my sister. It's a relief to tell her everything I've been keeping to myself since I wasn't sure how she'd take finding out my new beau is a kraken. It's good to catch up with her and have my secret mating out in the open with everyone who matters. Caroline knowing about it makes Kirby and my relationship seem more tangible. The weight of guilt at hiding something so important lifts from my shoulders.

When I step outside to start up the grill, Caroline turns her full focus onto my mate, but I'm not concerned about that. Kirby can hold his own with my sister. He's already charmed her kid, so that's enough to garner some major points in his favor with her. And I suppose the gooey heart eyes she catches me watching him with don't hurt either. She really does just want me to be happy, and she's taking the whole sea monster thing in stride. That's classic Caro. Always ready to take on anything for the ones she loves.

Hoyt arrives with his sister, Lida, and his niblings in tow as I finish cleaning the grill and start it preheating. He gives me a hug and offers to carry out the food. Kirby seems to be an effective seagull deterrent, so our meal should be safe from avian predation. Though I still don't entirely trust the food unattended until Kirby joins us on the patio. Lida brought a fruit platter and Hoyt secures his favored uncle status with an assortment of cookies.

We introduce our respective sisters and their kids to each other. Kirby plays the gracious host at my side, making sure everyone has drinks and knows where the facilities are. Normally, even a mild October day would be too cold for a dip in the Atlantic, but we're on the tail end of a heat wave. So it's warm enough that a dip in the surf is tempting. I've barely got the food on the grill when the kids ask to change into swimsuits so they can jump into the ocean. Kirby volunteers to keep them safe from unseen currents.

Caroline and Lida accompany their children into the water along with my mate. I overhear Hoyt's sister reminding the twins that their dryad abilities extend to communicating with sea plants as well as their terrestrial cousins. "If you get in over your head, or feel at all unsafe, reach out to the local kelp for a helping frond, alright?"

Both girls nod, their blond plaits bouncing in the dazzling late afternoon sun. It will set soon, what with my backwards sleep schedule, but for now we are all enjoying the day. Hoyt and I shoot the shit as the others enjoy the water. I can't tear my eyes off how well Kirby handles having three little scallywags clamoring all over him.

The three kids are getting along famously. They splash in the surf and shriek in delight when Kirby wraps them in those big strong limbs that can toss me around like I'm weightless. He flings them into the waves, then plucks them back up before they can struggle. It's hard to ignore how naturally Kirby interacts with them all. He always has a tentacle ready to catch any of them if they get in over their heads.

He mentioned that we could have kids together through the magic of the sea sorceresses, but he hasn't brought the topic up again since. Watching him with the children, I can't help wondering if that's something he might want for us someday. Maybe I'm not as opposed to being a dad as I once thought, if Kirby is their other father.

If not for his presence, I'd be more nervous about having the kids in the water here. The realtor made it clear that this cove isn't the safest spot for swimming, but I trust Kirby not to let any of the children come to harm. If he can return a lost toddler from the open ocean, this should be child's play, so to speak.

"You planning on flipping those burgers, Tris?" Hoyt asks, nudging me aside and taking the grill tongs from me when he notices me staring out to sea.

"Sure, be my guest, oh great griller." I snark at him. I'm not really mad about sharing the task.

"Don't mind if I do. I don't like my meat turned into briquettes, unlike some people." Hoyt gives me a pointed look.

"Hey, it's not my fault that the BBQ has a perfect view of my mate showing off his aquatic prowess. That would distract anyone." I gesture to where Kirby is effortlessly surfing Lyle across the waves.

"Uh huh. You might be an adept cook and baker, but you need to work on your grilling skills."

I laugh. He's not wrong. "Or I can just invite you over to do it for me so I can enjoy the scenery."

As I speak, a car rounds the sharp turn from town. Kirby submerges himself, still playing watchfully with the kids, but out of sight.

"Any time. So, Caro took the news alright?" Hoyt asks, both of us watching the car cruise past. It's got out-of-town plates. Most of the locals don't come out this way.

"Yeah." I nod. "Other than dropping her coffee and a minor bit of yelling."

"Eh." Hoyt shrugs, but he's distracted. I catch him mouthing the license plate number to himself and shaking his head before adding, "She's entitled to a little freak out if you never gave her any warning."

"To be fair, she didn't even tell me she was visiting this weekend."

"Well, then you surprised each other and it all evens out." Hoyt smiles at me, but I can see the coiled tension in his muscles and the hard set of his jaw. He is worried.

"What?" I ask.

He shakes his head. "It's probably nothing. I just recognized that car from my tour a few days ago. There was something off about the driver."

"Off, like, he's a hunter?"

"Maybe. I can't point to anything concrete. That was just the vibe I got from him. We've had a lot of potential sightings lately." He sighs, and I can tell he's stressed. "I've told the girls to keep their plants quiet while they are visiting. You should also have Kirby lie low."

"I will. Thanks."

He smiles at me, warmer now, and bumps our shoulders together. "We'll make sure no one touches our cryptids."

My phone lights up with a message from Brad. He's sent me another audacious headline about animal attacks and speculation that there will be another victim on the upcoming full moon. That boy is going to get himself hurt. I should tell him to leave it alone. Or maybe have Hoyt take him out of a tour and talk some sense into him. But before I can, the kids' happy yells draw my full attention.

"Uncle Tris, watch me!" Lyle calls as Kirby balances him up out of the water standing on one foot.

Hoyt and I both look out over the waves to watch all three kids show off their cool new boogie boarding technique. That involves Kirby being submerged, so it looks like they are actually riding the waves instead of having a kraken's help to stay upright. Hoyt and I both join in our sisters' hooting and hollering for the kids, waving and giving all three of them huge thumbs ups.

For a few shining moments, my life seems pretty damn perfect. I get to share my home with my mate and my family by choice and by birth alike. It is really sinking in that I'm not dreaming about my ideal future; I'm living it. If not for those damn hunters and the pesky college boy coworker I can't seem to stay mad at.

It's not much longer before the food is ready and we bring it all inside to eat—better safe than sorry with Kirby being visibly a cryptid. I help bundle the kids in towels so they can dry off to eat. No hunter is going to touch Kirby, Hoyt's dryad nieces, or a single other cryptid in our community as long as we have anything to say about it. Now that I've found my family, I'm going to fight for them.

We crowd around my table to enjoy Hoyt's expert grilling. Lida and her daughters excitedly fill in Caroline and Lyle about the world of cryptids. Kirby curls a tentacle around my ankle, giving me a reassuring squeeze when he notices my worried expression. He suctions fresh marks into my skin as a welcome reminder that he's here for me, even when we're apart. Hoyt is right. We'll get through whatever is going on with the hunters together. With my kraken mate by my side, anything seems possible.

Thanks for reading Kirby and Tristan's book! If you enjoyed their book, I'd appreciate you leaving a review or rating to help other readers find their story at https://www.amazon.com/dp/B0CSBS2XC5.

And if you're curious about where Brad will find a monster of his own, be sure to grab a copy of Mainely Monsters #2, Pulling Me Under.

For all the latest news about my sales and new releases, be sure to subscribe to my newsletter: https://landing.mailerlite.com/webforms/landing/i2w6l7

OTHER WORKS BY ALEX SILVER

Mainely Monsters

Monster Romance
   Kraken Me Apart Book 1
   Pulling Me Under Book 2
   My Shadow and Me Book 3
   Moth to the Flame Book 4
   Love Song for a Siren Book 5

Hauntastic Haunts

M/M Paranormal Romance
   Dan's Hauntastic Haunts Investigates:
   Goodman Dairy *Book 1*
   Hawk Lake *Book 2*
   Ivarsson School *Book 3*

Joliet Asylum *Book 4*

Kapler Hotel *Book 5*

Free download links to the shorts are available in my FB group:

Drew's Haunted Hangout (*A Hauntastic Haunts Short Story 1*)

Rafael's Haunted Halloween (*A Hauntastic Haunts Short Story 2*)

Lee's Haunted Holiday (*A Hauntastic Haunts Short Story 3*)

Shift Work

Omegaverse MPreg Romance
  Papa Bear (M/X)
  Squirrel Trouble (M/M) (expanded edition)
  Trash Panda (M/M)

Merry Exmas

Contemporary Christmas Romance
  Christmas Carl (M/M) #1
  Christmas Angel (M/X) #2

Table Topped

Contemporary Romance
  Roll for Initiative (M/M) #1 Gui & Paz
  Charisma Check (M/M) #2 Theo & Jude
  Saving Throw (M/X) #3 Errol & Rene
  Plus One Bonus (M/X) #4 Max & Si
  Dump Stat (F/F) #5 Laura & Alice
  Party of Three (M/M/X) #6 Pia, Emil, & Gregor
  Balanced Party (M/M/X) #7 Pia, Emil, & Gregor

Summer of Adventures

Kinky Contemporary Romance
  Dungeon Master (M/M)
  Knotty Boy (M/M)
  Service Call (M/M)
  Picture Perfect (M/M)
  Puppy Love (F/X)
  Stud Muffin (M/M/M)

Psions of SPIRE

Urban Fantasy
  Shelter (M/M) Novella 0.5
  Bright Spark (MMMM)Book 1
  Bold Move (MMMM) Novella 1.5
  Keen Sense (M/M) Book 2
  Weak Link (M/M) Novella 2.5
  Quick Fire (M/X) Book 3
  Clear Sight (M/M) Book 4
  New Look (M/M) Novella 4.5

  A SPIREverse daddy kink standalone
  New Ground (M/M/X)

Shared Universe Series

Super U - Superhero Romance
  Super U: Rising Storm (M/X)

Final Days - Zombie Romance
The Willows (M/M GNC)

Anthologies

Playing With a Full Deck: Stories of Hope in Hard Times
All Amped Up (F/X hope punk)
Listen: The Sound of Fear
Haunt (M/M trans gothic horror)
Fix the World
Upgrade (gay trans cyberpunk)

About the author

Alex Silver (he/them) grew up mostly in Northern Maine and is now living in Canada with one spouse, two kids, and a lovebird. Alex is a trans guy who started writing fiction as a child and never stopped. Although there were detours through assisting on a farm and being a pharmacist along the way.

Visit me online at:

http://alexsilverauthor.wordpress.com/

Browse my entire book catalog at:

https://www.amazon.com/Alex-Silver/e/B07NPBW615

Join my Facebook group at:

https://www.facebook.com/groups/alexsalcove

Follow me on BookBub at:

https://www.bookbub.com/profile/alex-silver

Follow me on Twitter:

https://twitter.com/asilverauthor

Sign up for my newsletter for a free short story at:

And as always, consider leaving a review on Amazon or Goodreads if you enjoyed this book, reviews are of vital importance to independent authors, thanks!